ON THIN ICE

PIPER RAYNE

Cover design: RBA Designs

Line Editor: Love N Books

Proof Reader: Shawna Gavas, Behind The Writer

The Winter Games have begun...

I'm the life of the party. A little loud and some buzz kills might say obnoxious, but if you're around me I guarantee you'll have a good time.

Unless your name is Demi Harrison.

If that's the case, you'd act like I'm the devil incarnate and go out of your way to avoid me. Which makes zero sense because at the last Winter Classics I rocked her world.

Whatever though. I need to concentrate on winning gold anyway. I was at the top of the standings coming into the games, but since arriving in Korea I've lost my edge.

I was never one for superstitions, but I can't deny that there's only one difference between my previous medal winning games, and these ones—her.

I've pulled off amazing feats in the past, but getting Demi to agree to sleep with me throughout the games might require divine intervention.

ON THIN Ice

DEDICATION

To all the men who make us laugh.

Note to Readers: *We used Winter Classics instead of the trademarked names Winter Games and/or Olympics. We did take a few creative liberties as well.*

CHAPTER ONE

"It's duet night?" I ask the guy running the karaoke at the bar.

He nods, his attention fixed on the song requests in front of him.

"As in I have to find a woman to sing with?"

Now, anyone who knows me knows I won't have any trouble finding a sing mate, but I want to sing my usual "You Shook Me All Night Long" by AC/DC. That's how I get the women in the first place.

He clicks a few buttons with his mouse. "Sorry, come back tomorrow," he says in his Korean accent. A couple approaches the podium and he shifts his attention their way.

Shaking my head, I sit back down at the table with my friends.

"Why so glum?" Skylar puts a pouty face on like I'm two and scratched my knee.

"It's fucking duet night," I say.

"Oh," Mia whips her head in Grady's direction. "Let's sing."

Grady eyes Beckett, blowing out a breath. What, did he think he would do it for him?

"I prefer to watch," Grady says.

Mia tugs at his shirt, placing her head on his shoulder and batting her eyes. "Please."

He stares down at her and we could poll this entire table on whether or not Grady will agree and they'll all say the same thing. He will. Grady's totally pussy whipped at the moment.

"Fine." Grady stands and holds his hand out for Mia.

"YAY!" she screams, plucking her phone from the table. "I have to find the perfect song for us first."

The two of them disappear, leaving me with Ross and Rachel, aka Beckett and Skylar.

"Fucking asshole."

Oh yeah, and Demi, the girl who gives me death stares on the daily. She's currently directing that talent down at the phone in her hands.

"What's the matter?" Skylar bends forward on the table toward her friend.

This should be good. Everything in Demi's life is *sooo* dramatic. I lean back and sip my beer.

Focusing my attention around the room, I notice that the small space is filled with men and women cuddled up to each other. Then I look at our table.

Six people. Three girls. Three guys. Hmm...

"Is it fuckin' couple's night?" I interrupt. My bad mood over how my practice runs have been going since we arrived —shitty, in case you were wondering—seems to be affecting my mood tonight.

Classic Demi death stare commences.

"No." Beckett answers. I'm sure he really doesn't give a shit what's up with Drama Demi.

"Look around." I gesture with my arm to the room around us and Beckett's gaze follows.

"Well, we're not a couple." He actually points between him and Skylar.

"Sometimes I wonder how you can see the tracks." I shake my head.

His eyebrows scrunch. Seriously, never in my life have I met anyone so blind. I mean, look next to you, dude. I get if he doesn't want a relationship, but he's practically in one. The last time I saw either one of them date anyone else was over a year ago and that was short lived.

"Next up is Grady and Mia," the announcer says over the speaker and we all turn toward the stage.

Grady stands there while Mia bounces up and down, smiling down at her friends.

"Go, Rogue!" I scream except he's not really living up to his nickname right now.

The song starts and beer flies out of Demi's mouth. Skylar starts laughing while I hand a napkin to Demi who seems to be over whatever pissed her off a minute ago as she and Skylar dance in their chairs while watching Grady and Mia sing, "Don't Go Breaking My Heart" by Elton John.

I lean back in my chair, smiling because Mia is belting out the song, dancing around Grady as he stands there, singing the lines in a monotone voice. He can't even look at Beckett or me.

"We should be taping this shit," Beckett says, pulling out his phone.

Skylar looks over at her 'friend.' "Let's go next."

Beckett smiles and nods. "You pick the song."

Of course, he's the only guy I know who would be excited about singing a duet.

Grady and Mia's song fades, and Mia rises on her tiptoes pulling Grady's face to her lips.

"Thank you," she murmurs and his face lights up. After handing both microphones to the guy, he grabs her hips and hoists her up into his arms.

The two kiss the entire time they're coming off stage. At least he's going to get laid later for singing.

"Let's go." Skylar jumps up, grabbing Beckett's hand.

"Way to go, guys!" Demi claps, giving a high five to each of them.

"Yeah, great job, Grady. You didn't seem to be having as much fun as Mia," I point out.

He rolls his eyes. "I don't see your ass up there." He sits down and takes a large swig of his beer.

"I have no one to sing with."

Mia's eyes shift and if I had time, I'd reach across and put my hand over her mouth.

"Demi. You two sing together."

Demi says nothing.

"I thought she had some hot boyfriend," I say to Mia.

Demi's been raving about some guy she met all night—what a gentleman he is and how he's so considerate. He skis for the French team. As far as I'm concerned, he's the fucking enemy, but whatever.

Demi lifts her phone. "Guess not."

So, that was the bad news.

"What, he likes brie and you don't?" I smirk.

I think that's the fifteenth death glare she's given me tonight.

"Actually." She leans back, crossing her arms over her chest.

Damn it, her tits are so fucking perfect. The memory of

motorboating them last Winter Classics surfaces as clear as glass in my mind. Wouldn't mind doing it again, except she hates me now.

"You two have a lot in common, Dax," Demi snips. "According to his text, he'd like to take the games as a break —aka screw every female he can."

"Ah, assumptions and stereotypes." I down another gulp of my beer.

"All the more reason you two should do one," Mia urges.

I'll take Demi's silence as a no. Whatever, there's gotta be a single girl here who wants to sing with the hottest guy in the room.

"Beckett and Skylar are up," the announcer says into the microphone.

The two are all smiles. Beckett's line is first and he's dancing, his shoulders moving up and down as the two walk in circles around each other and pretend to be Estelle and Kanye West singing "American Boy."

"Look at Beckett, he's totally into it," Mia says to Demi, sliding onto Skylar's seat to get closer.

The two are cute. Like sugar-coated candy store cute.

I finish my beer and slide it to the middle of the table. Since I capped myself at two drinks tonight, I'm on to water from here on out.

The girl's heads are bobbing to the beat and they start singing along with Skylar in their seats. Then Mia stands, rounds the chair and starts singing American Boy to Grady. The guy can't even fight the smile on his face.

The song ends, and Skylar jumps into Beckett's arms.

"So much fun!" she screams as he lowers her to the floor and they find their seats.

"Looks like you two are next?" Beckett waggles his eyebrows.

I look around the room to find someone else who didn't know this was couples' night.

"That fucking asshole." Demi's gaze is set on the door.

A guy stands there with a girl hanging off him. Short skirt, tight shirt, overly made-up face and a bottle of hair-spray holding up her hair.

"Is that him?" Skylar asks, peeking around Beckett to get a better view.

"Yeah. Guess he sent the text right before he picked up his date."

His eyes sweep the room. He's probably checking out who else is here, in case the chick on his arm doesn't pan out.

Demi stares down at her drink, picking at her beer label looking glum and uncertain.

Fuck this.

The legs of my chair scrape across the floor. "Let's go."

Mia and Skylar smile over at me, and Skylar nudges her to go.

"No. I'm not singing. Especially in front of him," Demi says.

"Listen. I'm a more than a suitable stand-in. Show him what he's missing out on." I keep my hand outstretched.

She looks to the table, taking a silent poll from her friends. Then she stands up and takes my hand.

On the way up to the small stage, I swing my arm over her shoulders. She immediately tries to circle out. "You have to act like you're into it," I whisper to her.

She stops trying to flee.

"You found someone." The karaoke guy looks surprised.

Maybe I should strip my shirt off, so he can see exactly what I have to offer the female species.

"'Promiscuous,' by Nelly Furtado," I tell him.

Demi huffs, her mouth hanging open.

I wink because there's no halfway with me. We're going all the way on this one.

CHAPTER TWO

We step up on the stage, the colored lights flashing down on us. I never realized how hard it is to see the people down at the tables.

I step forward and motion for one of the guys sitting at the table closest to us to pass me the empty chair beside him. He does, and I place it in the middle of the stage, then guide Demi to sit down.

Giving a thumbs-up to the guy running the show, I grab one mic as the song starts and I approach Demi as I sing the words. I figure I may be the only one all in, but she surprises me and stands up when the girl's part comes on and stands chest to chest with me while I hold the mic near her lips.

Her hands slide down her sides as she lowers to the ground and back up. I grind my crotch into her as she lays her head on my shoulder, singing into the microphone. My dick twitches when she pushes me into the chair and then she bends over, looking at me through her legs as I sing my part. Slowly, her body twists up and down. I walk up behind her, circling my hips as I get near.

She places her index finger in her mouth and bites

down on it. When it shifts back to her part, I hold the mic in front of her again while her hands land on my chest, running up and down. All the blood in my body pools between my legs.

Shit, my dick needs to understand the halfway mark. I know we usually do everything full throttle, but he's not getting any satisfaction tonight. And no way do I want to be standing up here on stage in front of everyone sporting wood like I'm some thirteen-year-old kid.

By the time the song is over, I'm so charged up I could probably come with one stroke of my hand. Demi hugs me, and I do the old junior high move, keeping space between our genitals. On the slow pull back, her gorgeous green eyes looking at me with curiosity.

"Yeah." I back up, handing the microphone to the guy.

"Sorry," she snickers, covering her mouth, obviously I've lost some stealth moves since junior high.

"Whatever."

We hop off the stage and none of our friends have their arms up to give us a high five. They're all sitting there with wide eyes and their mouths practically hanging open.

"Good job," Mia says.

"You need to head to the bathroom," Grady laughs, glancing down at my crotch with a knowing look. Mia slaps him on the stomach. "What? That was fucking hot shit. Next time we're doing that song."

"Will you actually participate?" Mia rolls her eyes.

"If you're grinding on me like that, hell yeah." Grady tips his beer and winks at me.

I can't complain, the girl didn't even give me a full lap dance, yet I want to dig out my cash and make dollar bills rain.

"I need a drink." Without waiting for anyone to

respond, I head to the bar. "Double whiskey." The bartender grabs the bottle while simultaneously palming a glass. "Shit...no... water." Alcohol would make this situation worse and I need to adhere to my training. Two drink maximum per night.

The bartender is nice enough to unscrew the top of the water bottle, and I drink the cold water down my throat. I crush the plastic bottle and set it on the bar, placing some South Korean won on table.

"Nice dancing, Campbell," the guy Demi was dating says in his stupid French accent as he leads the girl he brought to a table with his hand on her back.

"What can I say, she knows where to find the good stuff."

His hand leaves the girl's back and he twists back around, stepping up to me. I stand in place, not at all intimidated by anyone, much less this skinny prick.

"You're sloppy seconds." The arrogant prick looks me up and down.

I exaggerate a clutched over belly-holding laugh and then pop back up, straight-faced. "You should really get your facts straight." I search to make sure Demi is nowhere around and inch forward until my lips are right by his ear. "She's back for the good stuff."

Now I know I'm full of shit, but this jackass doesn't. All he knows is she was grinding me up on stage moments ago. And the way he so easily tossed Demi aside when they were dating irritates me.

He shoots me a cocky grin. "You're no better than me. I've heard the rumors." Funny he says that when he has no idea that at the last Winter Classics, it was well known that Demi and I were messing around.

"You missed out on something good with Demi," I say.

He glances over my shoulder and I don't have to turn around. I can already feel her there. Reaching my hand back, I find hers and link our fingers, pulling her forward.

Demi remains silent but doesn't pull away from my side. Unlinking our hands, I possessively place my hand on her hip, my thumb rubbing along the open space between her jeans and shirt.

His eyes shoot to the motion and just to be sure he's aware that he fucked over the wrong girl, I place my lips just below her ear, my lips casting small kisses on her soft skin.

Demi being the rock star actress she is, she leans in and she must really be trying to convince this guy that he didn't fracture her heart an hour ago, because she's closing her eyes, reveling in my affection.

"Whatever, Demi. We were never serious," he mumbles.

"Whatever, *Julien*. Does it look like I care?" she rasps in a sexy, throaty voice.

My lips travel up the shallow of her throat and I twist her so we're flush against one another. Her head falls between her shoulder blades and I make my way up past her jaw until my lips are millimeters from hers. Frenchie is still standing there—he must be into voyeurism or some shit. Not that I mind having Demi in my arms again. I'd forgotten how her body just kind of fit with mine.

Going for what could be a ball cracking move if she objects, I allow my lips to land on hers. I'm tentative at first, just in case I need to make a quick getaway. But she doesn't pull away. Instead, it's her tongue licking against the seam of my lips. Her breasts push against my chest, and she rises on her tiptoes to get closer.

My tongue seeks hers and once they slide along

together, a burst of something erupts in my stomach. I don't know what the feeling was, but my hand finds its way to the back of her head because the last thing I can handle right now is her stopping this fake kiss.

A small moan escapes her parted lips and I desperately want to know if she's acting or if I actually illicit that sound from her, because damn if I don't want to groan and lay her down on the table, not caring who's watching us.

Just when I'm about to suggest we head back to the village, she pulls back, covering her mouth and looking to where Julien was moments ago, but the space is empty. She looks around the room, searching, but it seems like he left, which is what we wanted right?

"It worked," she smiles over at me, rising to her tiptoes and kissing me on the cheek. "Thanks, Dax."

Frenchie might be gone, but the table of our friends are all staring at us with flabbergasted slack-jawed expressions.

Disappointment rests in the pit of my stomach that Demi's moan was only to up the ante on our fake kiss, but then her lips move to my ear. "Meet me in the bathroom in five."

I knew it.

I do a mental fist pump. I'm fucking Dax Campbell, no women on earth could kiss me and not want more.

She lowers herself back down on her heels, watching for my confirmation. I give her a small nod and try to play it off like I could take it or leave it. Make no mistake. I'm taking it.

Turning on her heels, she heads back to our table with our friends where the girls swarm around her, while the guys' attention is still focused on me.

I hold my hands up in the air like I did nothing wrong, but they shake their heads and share an expression that says they don't buy my innocent act.

I can't blame them, I'm rarely innocent.

CHAPTER THREE

Not wanting my friends to know that I'm about to get some ass—ass they told me wouldn't come back my way—I head over to a table in the back near the bathroom, pretending to be on my phone. Like I have some important shit to handle.

With an eagle eye on Demi, I watch as she rises from her seat, and walks by me, her finger sliding along my table as her eyes remain straight ahead on her destination. I glance over at our friends to make sure they don't suspect anything. I'm not in the mood to deal with their bullshit tonight. None of them are paying any attention to this end of the bar, so I follow her into the unisex bathroom, back to a stall on the far wall.

She steps in and I slide in after her, shutting and locking the door behind us.

"What—"

She grabs my shirt before I can finish, pulling me toward her and smashing her lips to mine. We both fight for dominance until I position her head exactly where I want it and delve my tongue into her mouth without an ounce of hesitation. The sugary taste of her cherry schnapps and 7 Up makes her taste even sweeter.

She reaches under my shirt, up and over my stomach, around to my back, holding me to her. Like I'd go anywhere right now. We're breathing heavy when she pulls her mouth off of mine for a second. "I still hate you."

I grab her face, cupping her cheeks with my palms and hold her out from me. The wetness from our kiss glistens on her lips.

"Hate fuck? I'm game."

Her eyes smolder as her nails run down my back.

I cover her mouth with mine, not that she has any objections because her fingers are now resting on the button of my jeans.

I want to taste every inch of her. Is it all the same as I remember? My lips travel across her jaw, sucking her earlobe into my mouth. I'm still awed by the softness of her skin, especially with the tough exterior she portrays.

She unbuttons my jeans, sliding the zipper gingerly over my arousal and my back hits the stall door.

I am *sooo* ready for this.

She laughs, sliding her hand down my pants and under the waistband of my boxer briefs.

"Fuck," I murmur, my breath turning ragged as I groan.

Her soft hand strokes me, her thumb running the pre-cum around my tip. Though I know from experience that she gives great hand jobs and blow jobs, it's her eyes watching me that have me growing harder than ice in my pants. It's like she's looking for affirmation that she's doing something right, not knowing that one touch from her and I'm a goner.

If only I had time to really explore where this could go, but a bar bathroom with a table of our friends too curious for their own good just outside the door, means we don't have the luxury of time.

"I think we need to move a tad faster." My fingers manipulate the button and zipper on her jeans and I pull them down. "Skirts. You need to wear a fucking skirt."

She giggles again, removing her shoes to help me get her out of her jeans, and then putting them back on her feet. This isn't my first rodeo in a bar bathroom and although our clothing makes it difficult, we're not raising the white flag anytime soon.

"Maybe we should go back to the village," she says.

I stare blankly at her. "You got me this hard, we're finishing this."

"Okay." She smiles, and her hands start searching my pockets. Finding the condom in my front pocket—what can I say? I was a boy scout and the motto 'always be prepared' stuck—she holds it up in front of us, a grin from ear to ear.

As if her sex appeal wasn't already high enough, she tears it open with her teeth, pulling it out and then rolling it down my hard cock. She rises up on her toes and kisses me, the tip of my dick hitting her stomach.

I break the kiss, swivel her around and urge her foot on top of the toilet lid, spreading her open. My chest falls to her back and if only she was naked, our skin would be touching. She moves one arm back, gripping my neck and the tip of my dick teases her opening.

"Now. I need you," she pants.

I plunge inside of her and her gasp mixed with my moan echoes throughout the small bathroom. I place my hand over her mouth but she doesn't seem to care, her eyes fluttering and her breasts pushing out. Sliding my hand off her mouth and up the hem of her shirt, I caress her bra-covered tit, my thumb playing with her hard nipple through the thin fabric.

Her warmth I could handle, but as she grows wetter, a want emerges from my body, unable to have enough of her. Flexing my hips, I thrust in and out of her, my teeth biting down gently on her shoulder, her iron-fisted grip on my neck making sure I don't try to escape.

"I forgot how good you were," she murmurs, and a smile comes to my lips.

"Is that a compliment?"

She shakes her head, her eyes still closed, her chest rising and falling with rapid breaths. "An orgasm will be your compliment."

For a few more minutes, we continue fucking in a public bathroom, trying to keep our moans down. We're in a position that doesn't offer a ton of hand roaming, but I manage to move my hand off her tit to between her legs.

My thumb circles her hard nub, which is her undoing. She bounces off my chest, breathless as all the pent-up energy drains from all her muscles. Watching and feeling her release ignites my own and I pump into her, my body twitching as I come.

We stay in the same position as our breathing evens out. Just as I'm about to give her some space, she moves away from me. I suck in a sharp breath when my dick leaves her warmth.

Her back is rigid, and it looks like the old Demi is back. "That was a mistake." She slips her shoes off and grabs her panties and jeans, throwing them over her legs and putting her shoes back on.

"I wouldn't say a mistake." I dispose of the condom in the toilet, flushing all evidence of what just happened into the Korean sewer system.

"It's never happening again." She straightens her shirt.

I pull up my boxers and jeans, fastening them. "Sure. Whatever."

Her hand is on the lock and she glances over her shoulder. "Don't come out for a few minutes."

No shit babe. "This isn't my first bathroom fuck."

Her icy eyes narrow. "Don't remind me." She leaves, closing the door a little harsher than necessary behind her.

"Chicks, man," I mumble. "You give them the orgasm of their life and still they bitch afterward." I shake my head, sitting tight for a few moments before I open up the door and head back to my friends.

Once I round the corner of the back hallway, I find Grady's knowing eyes on me. There's a smirk is on his lips, and he's shaking his head as if he's silently saying, 'you're such a fucking moron.'

Maybe, but right now I'm one damn happy moron.

CHAPTER FOUR

"What happened to you?" Coach Fitzgerald stares at me slack-jawed.

"I don't know." I run the race over in my head, staring at the timer in Coach Fitzgerald's hand.

"For the past week you've been taking corners wide, your times have been increasing and now you beat your record from qualifiers." He shakes his red-haired head.

"I know I had a rough patch, but I *am* the best snow-board crosser out there."

Coach laughs, his hand smoothing down his beard. "Glad to see that downturn didn't hurt your ego."

I unclip from my board, looking back up at the course. "Maybe it's the course."

He shrugs. "Yesterday you flopped. Same course."

"Well, whatever it is, I'm crossing my fingers nothing changes."

Coach smacks me on the back. "Okay, let's go again."

I hop on the snowmobile with my board tucked into my lap as it roars up the slope. Once we reach the top, a few of the other snowboard cross guys are up there and since I'd rather size up the competition than fly down the track by myself, we all decide to do a trial run together.

Usually, we'd hear complaints from the coaches, but they're all at the bottom of the hill with timers in hand. They'll be pissed, but for me to know if I really have it back, I need to race with others.

We all clip into our boards, our hands on the handles, our boards up against the metal blocker, our hips already flexing back and forth.

"See you losers at the bottom," I say in jest.

The other two guys laugh, the metal gates fall and like horses at a racetrack, we unleash all our force to be first out of the gate.

I'm not a music guy when I'm competing. I like to hear the sounds of my competitors gaining traction on me. I don't want music to drown out the noise of the snow and ice under my board. If someone is millimeters from running into me, I want to know it.

We fly up and down the mounds, catching small amounts of air as we rush to get back down on the track because we're faster on the snow than we are in the air. One guy gets close to me on the inside curve of the last twist, our boards almost touching.

Bobbing up and down, I get out in front of him and when we sail over the last ramp, I know it'll be close at the finish line. The finish line in my sights, I'm first over the line, my arms raised up in the air.

Coach Fitzgerald a few others roll their eyes at us. "You could've injured one of yourselves," he says, but shows me the timer.

You'd think I won gold from the smile on my face because, by some miracle, I'm back.

"Fuck yeah!" I fist pump, unclipping from my board and throwing it up in the air.

"Whoa, whoa, whoa." Coach holds his hands up in the air. "You need to take it easy. Go get something to eat and I'll see you in the gym this afternoon."

I pick up my board and pull out my cell phone to text the guys. Celebratory salads for all. Dax Campbell isn't a loser bet anymore.

———

BECKETT RAISES his hand to flag me over at the restaurant. It's been our go-to place to eat since we arrived in South Korea. They serve American food and although I want to head into Seoul and devour most of the local food, I'm waiting until I have the medal around my neck.

I slide into my seat. "What's up?"

"You're the one who asked for this lunch date." He sips his energy drink, his coat swung over the chair next to him.

"You have prelims tomorrow?" I ask him.

Poor Beckett, the Classics start immediately, so the only good thing for him is that he's done early. My guess is he'll stick around for Skylar's events though.

"Yeah."

"How's it going?"

He nods, taking another sip of his energy drink. He's less enthusiastic than he usually is. Hell, usually Beckett is a 'don't sweat the small stuff' type of guy. The one with a smile on his face and a joke ready, but not today.

"Does that mean good or bad? I can't read you."

Our usual waitress, Soonil, comes by. No introduction, her pen poised to paper and her eyes fixated on me.

"Hey, Soonil," I pronounce each syllable the way she likes. She doesn't have much patience for me, but I tend to wear people thin at times. It's a gift. Not my fault if people don't have a sense of humor. "See, this is where you say, 'Good afternoon, Dax, how was training this morning?'" Not even the corner of her lips twitch. "Well, Soonil, thanks for asking. I actually had a great morning. I happened to beat my time from qualifiers."

Nothing.

"Oh, Dax, that's great. I'm so proud of you. How about a celebratory drink?"

Her face is stone cold like she's had too many Botox injections and couldn't move a muscle even if she wanted to.

"Well, thank you, Soonil, I'd love a water. My throat is kind of dry." I rub my neck, the bristle of my scruff pricking my fingers.

She jots down something on her paper and walks away.

"She's going to throat punch you one day," Beckett says. "She probably wrote down to poison the asshole's water."

I feign innocence. "Who? Soonil? She loves me."

Beckett shakes his head like he usually does around me. "She thinks you're a lunatic who has conversations with himself."

"Probably, so let's get back to you. Did someone steal your lunch?"

He picks up his energy drink and places it to his lips. "Jackass, you know how I am when I compete."

"Yeah, a fun suck."

He tips his bottle my way. "So, you're out of your funk, huh?"

Soonil walks up at the same time, a bottle of water placed in front of me. I look up at her. Still no smile.

"Yes, I am." I wink at Soonil. "Can I grab something to eat?"

She pulls her pad of paper out again, her pen poised just like before.

"Still not talking to me?" I ask.

She nods for me to go ahead.

"Okay." I glance at Beckett briefly. "Turkey wrap, hold the mayo and can I have two boiled eggs."

She nods.

"Boiled eggs?" Beckett asks.

"Protein man. You know what." I snap my fingers. "Soonil?"

She turns, her veil of straight, black hair falling from over her shoulder. "Can you grab my buddy some eggs too?"

She nods.

"Thanks, Soo," Beckett says, and she smiles. Actually shows all her teeth and smiles at him.

"What the fuck? Why does she like you?"

"Because I'm polite."

"You shortened her name and she didn't murder you with her eyes," I say, suddenly very interested in the way she interacts with other customers.

"Are we going to talk about the server or the fact you're back at peak performance?"

The smile I haven't been able to get off my face since I finished training takes the place of my scowl. "I'm back, baby." I raise up my palm and Beckett smacks it.

"Good to hear!" Beckett might get kind of worrisome before he competes, but he's always our biggest cheerleader, so he's genuinely happy that I'm not dragging ass down the hill.

"Hey, where's Grady?" I ask.

"He'll be here in a bit, but I think he's got people with him."

"Like who?" I ask, taking a sip of my water.

"Like his girlfriend and her friend."

"Demi?"

He shrugs. "Demi doesn't compete for a few days. They were at the gym."

"Shit, I'm headed there next. I guess I'm solo." I lean forward because if Rogue, aka Grady, hears what I'm about to say, he might kick my ass. "Is it just me or has Grady become a major buzzkill since the girlfriend?"

Beckett laughs, another roll of his eyes. "You're just pissed because he doesn't have time for your bullshit anymore."

"They're always in her room."

"You sound like a spoiled four-year-old."

"This is the time it's supposed to be fun. All of us guys hanging out. He's pinned to Mia like a strap-on, you and Skylar are still living in that damn friendationship bubble—"

"A what?" he asks, but luckily Soonil interrupts us with our eggs.

"Thanks, Soonil," I say, and she breezes right by to the next table where she...smiles. Fucking smiles at them.

"I'm just putting this out there...I *will* get that woman to smile at me before the Classics are over."

"Good luck with that." Beckett bites off half his egg and chews for a second. "Why do you think you're back? What did you do?"

Beckett is the most superstitious athlete you will ever meet. I could go through a whole list of things he's done when he's winning. We've had to endure the usual dirty socks, one time he had a seashell in his pocket that supposedly saved him when he got caught in a riptide back home. I've seen it a lot in athletes, but nobody is as bad as Beckett.

"I did nothing. I just got my game back."

He raises a skeptical eyebrow.

"It's not because I sang that song last night. It's not what I ate for breakfast this morning. It's not that—"

"You slept with Demi last night?" Both of his eyebrows go up now.

"What? No! That was just a bonus."

He sips his energy drink. "Do you remember the last Classics?"

"That I slept with her? Yes, I remember." I chuckle. "That was the best part of last night...I knew how to get her off. Hence how we finished so quickly."

He exaggerates a disgusted shake of his body. "I'm good without the details." He pauses, probably for dramatic effect. "What did you win last classics?"

"Did I sign up for Psych 101?" I look around the room. "Nope, I'm in a restaurant."

"Answer the question."

I roll my eyes. "Gold. I won gold."

He nods, his eyes widening. "You sure she's not your lucky charm?"

"Yeah, I'm sure." My voice lowers and Beckett smiles my way. Usually, I wouldn't remember shit from four years ago. I do remember almost being late to my finals when I'd been giving Demi a congratulatory orgasm with my mouth between her legs because she won silver. Then I came in first every race, ultimately claiming gold.

Fuck, maybe Beckett's right. I've been off my game since we arrived in Korea. And I have eaten most of the same food, done most of the same things. There's just one difference.

"Look, your lucky charm just walked in." Beckett eyes the door.

I swivel in my chair, coming eye-to-eye with Demi Harrison. Out of all the lucky charms in the world, why couldn't I just have a rabbit's foot? Why does it have to be the girl who wants to kick me in the nuts?

CHAPTER FIVE

"He's going to grab this one." I zip my jacket up to my nose, bury my hands in my pockets.

We stand at the bottom of the halfpipe after watching Grady's first run not go as great as he would have hoped.

"Definitely," Beckett says next to me. The guy's in a much better mood now that his event is over, and he claimed silver for slopestyle boarding.

"Hey guys, how's he doing?" Skylar and Demi come up and join us. Beckett instantly gives each of them a hug.

My hands stay tucked into my pockets as they smile and wave. Demi stays on the opposite side of Skylar, as far away from me as she can get. For the first time in forever, I'm hesitant to talk to her. Ever since Beckett brought up the damn lucky charm thing, it's been stuck in my head. I can't help but replay the entire Winter Classics four years ago and damn if he wasn't right. I slept with her before qualifiers and finals. Actually, she went down on me in the middle of the qualifiers during a break. Now I have to somehow find a way to persuade her to sleep with me again before my qualifiers in a few days.

"Oh, Mia!" Demi waves her hand in the air.

Mia and her brother, Brandon, head down our way, their parents in tow.

"Hey, we were up closer but I think I was making him nervous." Mia cringes.

I fist pump Brandon. "What's up, Salty?"

"Just crossing my fingers he can pull this one out." He straightens his black-framed glasses on his nose.

"Look who's up." Beckett nods toward the screen where Matt Peterson's face is prominently displayed. "This'll be the deciding factor. If he uses his Peterson's Bag of Nuts trick and nails it, for sure he'll win gold."

Peterson is another American expected to do well these games. Basically, he's Grady when he started making a name for himself. Instead of seeing him as the threat he is, my buddy has been giving him pointers. What can I say? Grady can be an idiot.

"He's got nothing on my man." Mia stands right at the edge of the oval, clapping her hands.

"You do realize if you go home with gold and he doesn't, things might be icy," I say, and Mia twists her head my way, narrowing her eyes and I'm left with a shiver from the sudden cold front.

"He's going to win," she says with certainty.

Brandon knocks me with his elbow.

"Shouldn't you be up in the announcer's booth?" I ask him.

"Not for finals. Only qualifiers."

"That's bullshit."

"It is what it is." He shrugs. "I'm just happy to be here." One corner of his lips lift.

"For sure."

The announcement that Matt Peterson is next up

booms over the speakers, so we all shift our gaze to the pipe. He starts his run, dips down and he's hitting every trick, catching great air.

Why the hell did Grady help him?

"There it is," Beckett murmurs next to me.

"Damn," Skylar says. "Great ride."

The crowd goes crazy. He comes right up to the fence, slapping hands. The kid knows his ride was enough to put him in first. As we stand at the bottom, watching the screen, I guarantee the group of us are praying and hoping the judges saw something we didn't. Something they can deduct points for.

The score goes up and the cheers get louder. Matt's holding his board up in his hands, pumping it up in the air.

Grady's next and to even medal at all, he's got to move up in the standings. While we're waiting, I catch Demi in my peripheral vision running lip balm over her lips. You'd never guess she is a skier based on how soft her lips and hands are. Damn, I can't help but wonder what flavor that lip balm is. Last Classics she was like Baskin Robbins with thirty-one flavors of lip balm.

She glances at me from the corner of her eye and then turns to look directly at me. Demi Harrison is never intimidated. At least not by me.

I smile, hoping to calm the seas and maybe make my approach, but she snaps her attention back in front of her.

"What's up with you two?" Salty asks, knocking me again with his elbow.

"Nothing."

"So, I can ask her out then?" There's no ounce of humor in his expression, which means no one has shared my past with her.

"Sure." I bite back my first thought which is to punch him in the face because it's ridiculous.

He laughs, slapping Beckett on the back. "Same ol' Dax."

Beckett turns around, Skylar staring on, looking like she's wondering what they're laughing about. Thankfully, Demi is busy talking to Grady's mom who won't stop bragging about her son.

"Jackasses." I move away from them, wrapping my arm around Mia. "He's got this," I wink, and she slides into my embrace, slapping me on the stomach.

"I know he does."

Grady's face and name show up on the screen. "GO GRADY!" she yells, nearly busting my eardrum as though he could hear her. Her hands are clapping nonstop, she's jumping up and down.

"You get he can't hear you, right?" I ask.

Again with the arctic eyes. "He knows I'm here and it makes me feel a lot better than biting my nails in silence."

I hold up my hands. "Okay, okay."

Grady comes down to his starting point, and we watch him do his usual OCD routine, fastening one mitten and then the other and back to the other before he's satisfied.

"Here he goes," she mumbles, and she squeezes her eyes shut for a second as he drops in. "This is yours, babe," she whispers. This is entertaining. I've never in my life felt as much stress watching someone else compete as she is. You'd think she didn't already win her own gold and that it was her up there. It's fascinating in a way.

He catches the air he needs, grabbing his board and the crowd starts clapping.

"There you go. Keep it up. The triple..." Mia talks to herself as we all fixate on Grady.

He slides up the other side of the pipe and nails the trick. "Way to go. Just a couple more."

"Do you always talk to yourself?" I ask.

She elbows me in the rib, quick and hard. "Ouch." I rub my side.

"That's it, another one," she whispers, her hands sewn together and her eyes closing every once in a while.

Grady's had an excellent run so far. He's got enough tricks with high technical points to win if he can land his next two.

"One more. You're the best. Don't stress. Do the trick and land like you do every day..." She's not even finished with the sentence before his board falls midway down the slope of the pipe.

Flawless, a flawless run. Mia starts screaming, clapping and jumping.

Grady rides down to the fence line and leans over. Mia grabs his cheeks, planting a kiss on his lips. "You did it, babe! It's yours."

He smiles and lifts his goggles, his gaze landing on the scoreboard. The waiting is agony. At least in my event, I know if I was the first down I'm probably pretty solid.

Mia starts talking to herself, strike that, she's talking to the judges.

"You know he was the best. Give him the points he deserves. He's the best boarder out there."

"Again, they can't hear you," I say, and she jabs me in the ribs again. Harder this time. "Jesus!" I grip my side. "I do have prelims in a few days."

"Then stop saying stupid shit," she bites back, her eyes never leaving the screen.

"Hello, it's Dax," Demi adds.

I turn my head to see she's putting on more lip balm. It's

torture I tell you, pure torture for her to coat those lips and I have no idea what flavor it is.

The crowd roars with applause, screams, and cheers and when I look over at Mia, she's gone.

She's jumped the fence line, tackled Grady who is now on the ground with Mia's lips attached to his. Checking the board, I see he's seated in first place. Gold is his once again.

"The son of a bitch pulled it off." Beckett comes up next to me, Brandon on the other side.

"Look at the happy couple," Brandon jokes.

We'll wait for Grady to be done talking to the press before we move over to congratulate him.

"See you guys later. We gotta run." Skylar hugs Beckett goodbye and gives Brandon and I a wave. Demi waves and then scurries behind Skylar. "Tell Grady congratulations!"

I pull out my phone. "Shit, I gotta go, too. Practice run." I fist bump the two guys. "Give him hell for making it so close."

They both laugh. "Good luck," Brandon says.

I nod and head out to prepare to win my own gold medal.

How I do today will prove whether Demi really is my good luck charm or not.

CHAPTER SIX

"Your start was shit," Coach Fitzgerald says, letting the timer fall to his chest.

I position my goggles on top of my helmet, not sure what the hell the problem is. It can't be Demi. It can't.

Damn Beckett for putting that shit in my head in the first place.

"You have one more practice run. Then I'm restricting you to inside practice."

One more time to try the course before I have to be on it to win my medal. *Fucking great.*

I hop on the snowmobile without a word to coach. He's not going to be happy because I already feel like this run will be shit.

Getting to the top, I get on the board, mentally put Beckett's crappy opinion to the back of my mind and only think about the course, visualizing what I need to do to get down it the fastest.

The gate flips down, and I jet my hips so fast, I think it was a great start. By the time I reach the bottom, the truth is on Coach's face. The timer drops again to his chest, his head falling forward in defeat.

"What's happened? What's changed?" He approaches me and I unclip my board again, waiting for my breath to even out.

"It's because I didn't get laid again."

"What?" He picks up his head, staring at me with drawn brows.

"Last Classics, I was messing around with this skier when I won gold. Before the last run, I nailed her in a bathroom the night before. She's my lucky charm and I might as well face not medaling because she'll never sleep with me again." I toss my board a few feet away.

Coach laughs, his hands smoothing down his red beard. "You're shittin' me, right? You're telling me that you're fucked up in the head because you didn't get laid? Go find someone else then."

I shake my head. "It has to be her. She's the only one I slept with last Classics."

"What about the other competitions leading up to this?"

I'm not sure what excuse I have other than I wasn't around her then. She's a skier, I'm a snowboarder. We weren't running in the same circles. Our only common friend is Skylar and it's not like I see her much in the off-season.

"She wasn't around." I shrug.

"So, she's in your head is what you're saying."

I flip off my helmet, tucking it under my arm. "Only since Beckett put the idea in there."

He's still shaking his head. "Well, I'm Irish so I do believe there's something to be said for luck."

"URGH!" I scream up the mountain. "She's going to crush my balls."

Coach laughs, slaps me on the back. "If you want to medal, I suggest you do what you have to do. I'll see you in the gym tomorrow morning at eight."

I nod. Fuck me. I look down between my legs. "I'll try to protect you guys."

But I'm not sure I can. I'm pretty sure getting Demi to play nice might involve handing my balls over to her.

I RAISE my hand to knock on her door.

I drop my hand.

I blow out a breath.

I raise my hand again.

I blow out a breath.

I knock and tuck my hands into my pockets.

Footsteps echo from behind the door. My heart skips a beat, my stomach churning.

Demi opens the door, the welcoming smile falling from her lips. "Dax?"

I'm momentarily speechless because she's in a tank top that's so tight her erect nipples are practically yelling 'tease me.' I swallow down the extra saliva in my mouth.

She raises her arms, putting her hair in a high bun.

Not helping.

"I'm sorry, were you sleeping?" I ask and clear my throat.

She cocks her head. "An apology for waking me?" She reaches forward, the back of her hand resting on my forehead. "No fever. What gives?"

"Can I come in?"

She stands in front of the door, her expression telling

me that she's trying to figure out why I'm here. If she only knew.

"Okay." She steps out of the way and I walk in.

"You sharing with Skylar?" I ask, finding pictures of Skylar's family on one of the nightstands.

Skylar's parents are heavily involved in her career, which is completely foreign to me since I got here on my own.

"Um, yeah." Her hesitant voice says she's still trying to figure out why I'm here.

"Can I sit?" I motion to the desk chair.

She nods.

"So." I crack my knuckles, pulling on my fingers.

"Dax, why are you here?"

I look up at her. There's no judgment or seething anger, which says this might be okay.

"I want to apologize. I don't know what I did exactly, but I obviously upset you."

She huffs, walking over to the cabinet to grab a sweat-shirt, zipping it up and covering the eye candy I was enjoying. "Now you want to apologize? Four years later?"

I thought I said a good thing, but the anger in her eyes can't be missed.

"What the hell did I do?"

She rolls her eyes, standing up and walking around the small room. I sit silently while she roams around and tightens her bun, fiddles with her phone, picks some lint off her sweatshirt, until I can't take it anymore.

"What? Demi? Just tell me what I did."

"You fucked me and left me," she snaps, stopping all movement. "You just left." Her angry tone fades and she fiddles with the strings of her hood.

"What? We were just messing around when the opportunity presented itself."

She shakes her head. "Not to my knowledge."

"We were having fun. You wouldn't want me as a boyfriend anyway. I'm not a relationship guy. Everyone knows that."

What is she thinking? I'm not the guy who will buy her a ride on some horse-drawn carriage or order roses with some sappy love note on Valentine's Day. I'm the freewheeling, take life as it comes, non-committal but fun while you're with him guy.

Still, I feel bad that we weren't on the same page all those years ago and that she ended up hurt because of it. I may be a playboy, but there's no enjoyment for me in making someone feel like a throwaway.

"I thought we were on our way to something." She turns her head and walks over to sit on the bed facing away from me. "But don't worry, I'm over it now, so thanks for the half-assed apology. You can go now."

I stand up from the chair, the squeakiness of the wheels making her turn in my direction to see me approaching. She sticks her hand out in the air and shakes her head.

"Shit. I'm a dick." I sit down next to her, my hand on her shoulder. "Demi," I say.

She's too busy shaking her head that I'm not even sure if she's listening to me. "It's fine Dax. I'm fine. It's probably just bugging me more right now because of everything that went down with Julien."

She turns her head and I catch the lone tear that falls with my thumb.

"I truly am sorry. I thought we were having fun for the Classics. I didn't realize you thought differently. But trust me, you dodged a bullet." I knock her with my shoulder.

She lets a small laugh escape.

"I'm not joking, you would've dumped me a week into it. I'd make a shitty boyfriend."

She smiles and rolls her eyes, though this time a little more playful.

"And why the sudden revelation?" She scoots back on the mattress and brings her knees up to her chest, effectively separating any closeness between us.

I shrug. "I really enjoyed the other night."

"I assumed you would."

"Did you not?" I ask. "The way your body responded, I think you enjoyed yourself as well."

She rests her chin on her knees. "It was nice."

"Nice? Nice is for middle-aged, married people."

She laughs again. I forgot how much I missed the thrill that runs through me whenever I can make her laugh. "It was great, Dax. The best I've had in the last four years. Better?"

"How about hot, earth-shattering, and you put me on speed dial?"

"Put you on speed dial?"

I take my chances, sliding a little closer to her. "How about we try this again? No strings. An agreement that it's just for while we're here."

"You're propositioning me?"

I raise my shoulders. "I'm not usually someone who goes back, but I have to say I kind of crave you."

"Like a candy bar?" She tilts her head and I stop my hand from tucking the loose strand of her strawberry blonde hair behind her ear.

"Like the most decadent chocolate in the entire world."

"Dax Campbell, did you just sweet talk me?"

"I can be sweet." I reach forward and tuck the piece of hair behind her ear.

Her gaze stays on me, deep in thought and I hope considering my offer.

"You can see other people, I don't care," I say just to sweeten the pot.

She studies me again. "I can see other people?"

"Yeah."

"And what about you?"

I shake my head. "Only you. I only want you."

"Those are words a girl loves to hear but not necessarily in this capacity." She smiles showing she doesn't mean it in a bad way.

"What can I say? I'm a closet romantic."

There go her eyes again, rolling to the back of her head. "Well, I'm not exactly looking for any type of relationship after my most recent experience and the sex between us is a great way to ease some of the pressure of the games, so what the hell? Okay."

"Okay?" I ask, biting my lip and double-checking.

She nods. "You must've caught me at a weak moment."

"So, can we get this started now?" I slide closer, my hands moving her legs apart.

"I was taking a nap..."

She doesn't fight me and her legs part, opening for me to slide between as my lips move to hers.

Just as I'm about to taste the latest flavor of her lip balm a finger lands on my lips. "Dax?"

My eyes open. "Yeah?"

"This is over when I say so, okay?"

"Of course. You're the boss." I press my lips to hers, and she doesn't stop me this time.

In fact, I'd say she was jonesing for me as much as I was

for her because she flips me on my back, straddling me and stripping off her sweatshirt and tank top.

My hands instantly mold themselves to her straining tits and I bite my lip from the image in front of me.

Where's a camera when you need one?

"I'm a fucking genius," I say, and she giggles as she falls on top of me, her lips crashing into mine.

CHAPTER SEVEN

"So, you took my advice," Beckett hops on the treadmill next to me.

I look to my left. "I have no idea what you're talking about."

"Demi? Your lucky charm."

I whip my head behind me to make sure no one is around. "We've come to an agreement, yes." I up my incline.

"That's what I heard. You couldn't commit to trying a relationship?"

I distort my face so he knows I think he's crazy as fuck. "I'm not a relationship type of guy. Don't enter the jewelry store unless you're buying a ring."

"You really need to work on your idioms."

"Do you not understand what I'm saying?" I click up another level on my incline, my thighs already feeling the usual burn.

"I get what you're saying because I'm your friend, but—"

"You do know you're in a relationship, right?"

Beckett glances over, grabbing his water bottle and

taking a swig. "Then someone should tell my dick because it's not getting any action."

"That's exactly my point. You have all the responsibilities of one and none of the fun."

The sound of our feet pounding on the treadmill echoes out as he's quiet for a minute before responding. "And you think you're getting all the fun and no responsibilities."

"What's up guys?" Grady hops up onto the machine on the other side of me.

"What am I missing? You two shitheads are done with your events. You should be banging your girlfriend and you should be banging your pseudo girlfriend," I say to them, my head volleying between the two.

"I'm not resting until you're done. What do we have, four days?" Grady asks, instantly accelerating to his jogging rhythm. The man is a machine I swear.

"Qualifiers in four, finals in five. How is it that Demi and I got screwed this year? She competes on the second to last day."

"Hey, last time it was me." Beckett points to himself, grabbing the hem of his shirt and wiping his face.

"So, we all celebrate after. The night of the closing ceremony," Grady says.

I shake my head at the two of them, clicking the incline button another time. "If I were you guys, I'd be locked in my hotel room with room service delivering on the hour and my girl naked next to me."

Grady laughs. "Nice friend you are." He looks past me to Beckett.

They know I'm full of shit. There isn't much I wouldn't do for the guys on either side of me.

"Is your family coming?" Beckett asks, he's about the

only one who can ask me questions like that because he has as many family issues as I have.

"Nah. They'll watch on the television."

He nods and lets the topic die there where it should.

"Mia and I are heading into Seoul tomorrow. Any takers?"

Beckett's eyes light up. "Me and Sky were thinking about it, too. Supposedly, Demi's got two tickets to some Korean game show."

"What?" I whip my head in his direction and he laughs.

"What the hell? Did I just say fried chicken or some shit?"

Grady laughs. "Man, he really must be missing all that junk food."

"Have you guys seen the Korean game shows? I gotta score a ticket." I pluck my phone out from the holder. I'm a master at texting and running.

"Since you're her orgasm inducer I'm fairly sure you can get one," Beckett says.

"What's this? What am I missing?" I feel Grady's eyes on me, but I'm too busy texting to care.

"Oh, let me fill you in, Rogue." Then Beckett starts telling him everything that he heard from Skylar, who heard it from Demi.

Me: *I just heard a rumor about you.*

Demi: *Well, I am fabulous so I'm not surprised people are talking about me.*

Me: *You're gorgeous, smart, funny, and sexy as all hell.*

Demi: *... Dax? What do you want now?*

I laugh.

Me: *I heard you have two tickets to a game show in Seoul?*
Demi: *I should've known you only compliment me when you want something.*
Me: *Wrong. I told you what a great ass you had the other day right before I slapped it.*
Demi: *Semantics*
Me: *And what about when I said I loved how tight your pussy is?*
Demi: *Okay, okay... the ticket is yours. How do you expect to pay?*

I can practically hear her purring in her text.

Me: *I'll be over in an hour. I'm assuming some quality time between those delectable thighs will be an acceptable form of payment?*
Demi: *That's a start.*
Me: *Be there in an hour.*

I DROP my phone back into the holder on the treadmill, both my buddies staring at either side of my face.

"What?" I ask.

"Nothing," Beckett says, shaking his head.

"Not really worth a conversation." Grady slows the treadmill. "He'll only deny it."

Beckett slows his, too, and soon they're each walking away from me.

"See you, Soups," Grady says.

"What the fuck? What just happened? What happened to sticking together?"

I'm screaming to myself because they stop and talk to a few other athletes heading into the workout room.

Whatever.

I up my incline again, increasing the speed. The faster I finish this workout, the faster I'll be buried deep inside of Demi which is the only place I want to be right now.

———

I KNOCK ON HER DOOR. Footsteps pad across the floor and the door opens. I step in and reach my hands out to grab the woman's hips.

"Ugh, no." Skylar puts her hand up in the air. "We're really not hard to tell apart."

I walk past her and throw myself on the bed.

"Where's your roommate? I need to pay her."

"Ew, I don't want to know." She busies herself at her desk, packing up a bag.

"You didn't mind sharing all our sordid details with Hoff."

She twists around, resting her back on the desk, crossing her arms over her USA sweatshirt.

"You wanna know what I think?"

I lean up on my elbows, my ankles crossed.

"I think that the two of you are playing with fire." She points her finger at me. "I think that you'll hurt her again. I love you, Dax."

"Awe," I place my hand over my heart. "I love you too, Skylar."

She rolls her eyes.

"I love you, but you're like a four-year-old some-times. Pushing and bulldozing your way through life without caring about who or what you've left in your wake." She grabs a backpack and hitches it over her shoulder.

I sit up and stare directly into her eyes. "If you think that, you don't know me at all."

"Maybe I don't. It's just been my observation and I think this is all fun and games right now, but in the end, it'll be Demi that's destroyed."

Demi walks in, her cheeks rosy from the cold. "What?"

"Hey, Beckett and I are going to catch a hockey game. I'll be back later." She pats her friend's shoulder while looking at me.

"Have fun," Demi says, removing her gloves and hat, depositing them on the table.

"Give your friend my best. Maybe spend the night, but that's probably crossing the line, right?" I sneer. If she's going to throw daggers, I'll throw them back.

"Bye." Skylar shuts the door.

"What was that?" Demi asks, unzipping her coat.

I lay back down on the bed. "Nothing. I'm here to pay my debt."

She smiles, the one where her entire mouth opens and shows all her white teeth. The one I don't get to see nearly enough.

"Yeah, sorry, I was just getting off the hill when you texted me. I have to shower quick. My mom, ugh, she just won't let me rest for a moment."

"Pushing you, huh?" Guessing that we won't be getting down and dirty under the sheets for a while, I sit up and rest my back on her headboard.

She hangs up her jacket and then bends over to take off her boots. God, her ass is on point.

"She expects perfection, you know? Like I get it that she medaled in three Classics and that she's an excellent skier, but I have coaches. Coaches that are a hell of a lot more patient with me."

Off go her socks, and then her shirt.

I sit back admiring the strip show she's giving me without her realizing.

Her thumbs hook into her yoga pants. "I mean, does she think I'm out there trying to fuck up? I'm flying down a hill at seventy miles per hour. I want to say yes, I did that move so I could straddle the line between paralyzation or death. UGH!" She stands there in only her bra and panties. A matching blue set that makes my dick twitch in my pants.

"Your mom just wants you to do well."

She looks me directly in the eyes, her two hands reaching behind her back and then the blue fabric glides down her arms until she throws it into her hamper. "For her or me?"

Her nipples are hard and ready for me, and my mouth salivates, wanting so badly to lick the budded peaks.

"You. I'm sure it's for you," I say when she doesn't respond.

She shakes her head, her hands sliding her panties down as she steps out of them, throwing them to join her other dirty clothes.

"Come here." I hold my hand out for her.

She takes the elastic out of her hair, the long reddish strands falling over her freckled shoulders.

"I'm dirty and I probably smell."

I grab hold of her hand and yank her to me.

"Did you really think you could strip in front of me and I'd just sit here and wait for you to shower?"

Her million-dollar smile warms her face. "You could join me."

"I was wondering when you'd ask."

CHAPTER EIGHT

The hot water feels like heaven as it streams down my back, but an even better feeling is my face between Demi's legs. With one of the smallest showers known to man, we had to be inventive. Her one leg is propped up on the bench, her back is flat against the wall with one hand fisted in my hair.

"Don't stop," she cries out right when I flatten my tongue and suck her clit into my mouth.

My scalp burns from her pulls on my hair, but that only spurs me on to make this experience that much more groundbreaking. Taking one hand off her thigh, I push a finger in and out of her in a quick motion.

"Ohh," she moans.

I look up from between her legs to find her eyes closed. Hopefully all that shit her mother is putting her through is long forgotten.

My tongue twirls her clit around in my mouth, and I plunge a second finger inside of her.

Her body rises and then falls from surprise and her hand moves off my hair, reaching and grasping for anything to hang on to. She finds a soap dish, her knuckles white from gripping it so tight, and I smile up over her mound at her.

Now is not the time to make this semi-climatic so I focus back on my goal, swinging her leg over my shoulder so both my hands are free, I slither my free hand up her ribcage until it finds her tit. Rolling her nipple between my thumb and forefinger is her undoing. She hits the tile wall, grinding into my mouth and hand, moans and groans tumbling from her lips.

"Dax," she sighs, her breathing rushed and hiccupped.

Not about to move my mouth, I keep doing what I'm doing so I don't mess with her orgasm. One minute later, the soap dish she was gripping falls to my feet and she clings to the showerhead.

"You're so fucking good." All the tension evaporates from her stiff body.

I slow my motions to let the waves of her climax retreat, then I lower her leg to the ground, raise up and cup her cheeks and let her taste herself on my tongue. She kisses me back, her fingers weaving through my blond hair as I pull her body flush with mine.

Moments later, I draw back, resting my forehead on hers. "Payment accepted?"

She giggles, her green eyes lighting up. "Yeah. Payment definitely cleared."

An hour later, we're getting dressed. "You wanna head to the hockey game?" Demi throws on her sweater, covering up the body I just devoured for the past hour.

"Who's playing?" I ask, bending down to put my socks on.

We haven't really been doing anything outside the bedroom and I'm a little nervous that an outing together could set us back to square one. She always seems annoyed by my humor unless—she's about to get laid—she might very well push me off a mountaintop if I gave her the chance.

"Canada and I don't remember who, but it might be fun. Competing at the end of the Classics kind of sucks, you know?"

I couldn't be in more agreement. The waiting and still training while our four other friends are done and soaking up the sights blows.

"Kind of wish I'd planned to stay back a few days," I say, straightening my shirt.

She buttons her jeans and then sits down in front of the mirror, putting on her makeup.

I guess she's going whether I go or not. I don't know why that bothers me. It shouldn't.

"You still could." She closes one eye to put liner on.

"Not really, I have to get home."

She turns in her seat, pushing and pulling a mascara wand in and out of the tube. My dick twitches for what reason I don't know. I just blew a load.

"Is your family not coming?" she asks.

I put my shirt on, and button my pants. "No. They like to watch from home."

Simple, right? She studies me for a minute and I try to keep my face as straight as I can. Like it's no big deal.

"Oh. I wish my mom had stayed home."

Grabbing my jacket, I swing my arms through the sleeves. "Ah, she loves you."

She finishes putting on her mascara, stands and goes to the dresser. Fishing out a pair of socks, she sits back down, pulling her legs to her chest. I smile at her toenails that are painted into little American flags.

"I meant to tell you, nice toes."

A soft blush creeps up her neck. "Thanks. They'll be ruined by the end of the Classics, but I do love them." She wiggles them before covering the masterpieces with her socks.

I pull up the information for the game on my phone. "Canada versus Sweden."

She looks up to me for a second, puzzled.

"The hockey game."

She shakes her head and smiles. "Sorry, my mind kind of drifted there for a second."

Grabbing her boots, she steps into them and then pulls her coat from the hanger. "You game?"

I nod. What else am I gonna do tonight?

"As long as we don't sit by Skylar and Beckett, I'm cool."

She shoots me that puzzled look once more. "Let's go then."

I open her door and hold my hand out for her to go first.

"Such a gentleman."

"Don't get too used to it."

She giggles and falls into step with me. "I'd never expect anything from you, Dax, don't worry."

Her words hit me, right in the fucking gut. I take a break from putting my gloves on to cover my stomach with one hand. What the hell was that?

CHAPTER NINE

"GO CANADA!" Demi screams, standing up in her seat, her fist raised.

"You do know they're our competitors, right?" I lean back into my nosebleed seat. This is what happens when you decide an hour before the puck drops to come see the gold medal hockey game.

She looks over her shoulder. "We don't play hockey."

"Yeah, well I got a Canadian riding my ass this Classics."

She plops back down after Sweden slaps the puck the away from their goal line. "They're North America, right?"

I shrug. She's got a point I suppose. And here I thought my only entertainment in coming here would be the fights and maybe ruining my diet with nachos.

"You have to cheer for someone otherwise it's boring." She pops a piece of popcorn in her mouth.

She surprised me. Her diet's gone to hell since we've been here. She's even halfway through a beer.

"Do you diet?"

She looks over to me, narrowing her eyes then crossing her legs and leaning in close. "Do you think I need to diet?"

I can't help but laugh at how cute she looks right now. "No."

She nods. "Good answer." She places a piece of popcorn on her tongue and pulls it back into her mouth. That delectable mouth that holds the tongue that twirls around dick like it's an ice cream cone.

Damn. Once again, I'm ready to go.

"If you mean do I not eat junk food. Yeah. My mom manages my diet most times and I'm like a teenager when she's watching me." She leans in close to me again, the scent of the watermelon from her lip balm lingering around us like an aphrodisiac. "I have a secret drawer," she whispers.

"Most girls have a drawer of sex toys. You have a drawer of candy?" I raise my eyebrows, my arm slung over the top of her seat and she leans back, propping her feet on the back of the seat in front of her. We could move three rows up, and I'm not quite sure why we didn't. But the privacy is nice back here. We can actually talk. Truth is I don't know that much about her. Like the mother thing. I'd heard that her mother helped advise her and I just assumed she wanted it that way since she was a medalist herself, but I'm getting the idea that that's not the case.

"I didn't say I don't have two secret drawers." She waggles her eyebrows. Poorly I might add, but either way, she looks adorable.

"Maybe we should explore them."

"Why, Mr. Campbell, do you want a candy bar?"

I grab a piece of popcorn and throw it at her forehead. She mocks offense and then grabs one and throws it at me.

"Two points." I chew and swallow the kernel.

"UGH!" She grabs a handful and tosses them at me.

A couple hours later, we leave the arena after Canada's win. Demi's voice is hoarse from screaming, and my stomach is not too happy with the nachos I shared with her. Both of us are a tad buzzed from the few beers we had.

"Here I thought I'd be a bad influence on you," I say.

She laughs, knocking her shoulder into my side. "You are a bad influence."

I swing my arm around her shoulders, not letting her pull away. "Agree to a tie?"

Her shoulders rise and fall. "I suppose."

"You suppose? You just convinced me to drink beer and eat nachos."

She laughs, and her head falls to my shoulder. "You loved every second of it."

I can't argue so I plead the fifth with my silence.

My phone dings in my pocket and I pull it out seeing a picture from Beckett.

"We were spotted." I hold it out in front of her.

"They're like little spies." She yanks the phone from me, zooming in on the picture.

Looks like they snapped it when I couldn't stand it anymore and pulled Demi in by the back of the head until our lips met. Her cheerleading was too damn cute, and I craved her more than I usually do. Which is to say a hell of a lot.

"What are they, the kiss cam?" She hands me back my phone, disgust clear in her tone.

"Skylar doesn't approve, huh?"

She glances over to me, the light her eyes have been filled with all night dimming a little. "She thinks you're a heartbreaker." She makes it sound like a joke, but I can tell it bothers her.

I'm really enjoying my time with her, but if she truly does get hurt in the end, I'm not sure it'd be worth it.

"Hey." She knocks her shoulder to mine unexpectedly and I stumble sideways before regaining my footing. "Don't worry. Skylar always plays it safe. Look at her and Beckett. The two of them should obviously go on at least one date to test the waters, but they won't even chance it."

I nod in agreement, but I did hurt Demi last Classics. So much so that she loathed me.

"I'm serious, Dax. No worries on this end." She holds her hands up in the air. "I'm in this strictly for the benefits."

I stop us before we reach the village. "You'll tell me if that changes at any point?"

"It's not going to, so, how about a quickie before we go our separate ways?" She does the whole waggling her eyebrows thing again which only makes me laugh.

"You do speak my language."

"I speak Dax?" she asks with a smile, walking in front of me, sashaying her ass.

Doesn't she know she doesn't have to tempt me? I'm already hers.

CHAPTER TEN

"You qualify in two days, right?" Demi's across from me on the train as we zoom to Seoul for the night. The train is crazy fast and even for an adrenaline junky like myself, it's a tad scary.

"Yeah."

"Nervous?"

"Never." I manage to say it with a straight face.

"Liar."

"Maybe." I shrug.

She smiles, kicking me lightly with her foot. She's wearing leggings, boots, and a long sweater. Her makeup is a heavier than it usually is tonight, and she's replaced her lip balm with lipstick. That kind of upset me. I like to explore all the flavors of the rainbow on her.

"You're always hitting and kicking me." I push my boot back on her leg, nudging it.

"Does it bother you?" She digs in her purse, pulling out a pack of gum.

"I'm used to being messed with. Two older brothers."

She continues to watch me, obviously expecting more information. "And…"

I raise my eyebrows. "And that's it. I'm the youngest of three."

"Mom and Dad?"

"Mom."

Like she's done many times, she studies me, like she's trying to figure out all the answers to what makes me tick. "Okay." She lets it go, which somewhat surprises me, but like she said last night, she doesn't expect a whole lot from me. I've always appreciated that from women, but with this one, it bothers me.

"I'm it in my family," she says.

"Quit after you huh?"

"Because you can't improve upon perfection." Her lips turn up and she tucks one side of her hair behind her ear.

"Well, mine kept trying and they never achieved perfection."

"Oh, I don't agree with that." Her foot kicks my leg again. "They have a gold medalist."

It's not the bragging rights my family enjoys, it's my money.

I switch seats, sitting down next to her. "Wanna make-out?"

She draws back, her head knocking on the train wall. "There are people around."

I take in everyone around us. The closest couple has their backs to us. "No one's around." I slide closer and her hand lands on my chest.

"Trying to distract me?"

I nuzzle my head into the crook of her neck and she moans. "Is it working?" I whisper in her ear.

"Maybe." She wraps her hands around my neck and turns her body, welcoming me into her personal space.

My lips move up her neck, my tongue searing a path to her earlobe where my teeth find the small piece of delicious flesh to nibble on.

"You're bad news," she jokes, her fingers playing with my hair.

Capturing her lips with mine, my hand glides up the outside of her leg, lifting both over my lap and I slide a tad closer.

I lick the seam of her lips and she opens for me, her tongue pushing into my mouth and when our tongues touch, an electric current courses through my body. I worried that Demi would still be standoffish with me when we were hanging out. The last Winter Classics we kept it strictly to the bedroom. We would meet up at one of our rooms, screw and then go our separate ways. There were no hockey games, no trips to Seoul, and there definitely wasn't any talking about our private lives.

With my hands on the curves of her body, our tongues entwine in a slow, easy kiss. I can't help feeling like things are different this time. Like we're developing a friendship, accepting each other and actually enjoying each other's company.

I close the kiss, my head moving back a little to see her swollen lips and flushed cheeks. All I want is to move back in, stay glued to her for the entire train ride. Truth is I'd rather rent a hotel room and forget the show, especially after discovering that even though she's not wearing her Chap-Stick, her lipstick does, in fact, have a flavor. "Strawberry."

She smiles, her hand still rubbing along the back of my head. "Bingo."

With her legs over mine and her hand in my hair, to an

outsider, we look like a couple. That's exactly why I mentally reprimand myself for initiating the make-out session. I can't lead her on and I won't hurt her.

"Make-out session done so soon?" she asks, swinging her legs back in front of her and off my lap.

Maybe she's on the same page as me. If she liked me that way she would've stayed in that position to be close to me. I've had girls who couldn't accept that we'd be nothing more than fuck buddies. They usually keep their hands on me as much as possible, using the excuse of sex when in reality they're looking for the affection a boyfriend would give them.

Demi pulls out her phone, her thumbs going a mile a minute with a smile on her face like it really makes no difference if our make-out session ended or not. Huh.

THE GAME SHOW was kind of a bust, probably because neither of us speak Korean and we're used to reading subtitles at home.

"I thought it'd be better," Demi says as we exit the early taping.

"Maybe if we understood it more." I open the door for her and we walk out to the streets of Seoul.

"True. Why did I think they'd have subtitles on a screen for us or something?"

"Let's chalk it up to our brains are fried from training."

She hits me with her shoulder. I'm really starting to like these little hits now and then from her. "Yep, let's go with that."

My stomach growls and she glances over.

"Hungry?"

"Starved."

"Me, too."

She looks around. "What do Koreans eat for a late breakfast?"

I try to spot something familiar. "Let's start walking. There has to be something."

She starts down the sidewalk and I quickly catch up to her. We're in the middle of a shopping area when I see a line for a street vendor.

"Let's go there."

She looks back at me, her eyebrows crinkled and raised. "Um..."

I tug on her jacket. "Come on. Live dangerously."

She willingly comes, although begrudgingly. "Do you eat from the vendors in New York City?"

I position us in line, a few people turning their heads and giving us the up and down, probably assuming we could be athletes for the Winter Classics. No one asks us though.

"I don't go to New York very often, but I would."

For the first time in the last few days, the Demi I always assumed she was appears. She's apprehensive, on edge and definitely isn't game for eating from a cart in the middle of Seoul.

Leaning in close, the scent of strawberry from the new layer of ChapStick she applied when we got out of the game show building awakens my sexuality. "It wouldn't be this crowded if it was poison."

Usually that line would earn me a little slap in the stomach, but instead, her hands stay tucked in her jacket. She gives me a quick nod.

I tug on her jacket again, stepping out of line. "Come on."

She doesn't move.

"We'll go somewhere you're more comfortable with."

One guy leaves with five sandwiches wrapped in paper.

"I'm good. Let's just get this, but then I'm torturing you while I shop."

I stare up at the big mall in front of us, my body already feeling limp from exhaustion.

"Anything but shopping."

She smiles, and that timid Demi leaves briefly until we're standing in front of the street vendor again.

"Four Tost-u." I raise four fingers in case the guy doesn't understand English. I really meant to learn Korean before this Classics, but time kind of got away from me.

The man hands us four of the sandwiches, I pay and leave the rest for a tip.

"Kamsa-Hamnida," Demi says, bowing her head to the man.

"Chaman-hey-yo," he says back, a grin tipping the corners of his mouth in a surprised and appreciative manner.

We walk to a nearby bench, with only one spot open so I motion for Demi to sit.

"You speak Korean?" I ask, handing her a sandwich.

"Jom." She places her hand up with her fingers slightly apart.

"I should've known." I take a huge bite of my sandwich. Delicious.

She laughs, staring at the sandwich like it's a cow's tongue or something. "Should have known what?" She picks up the sandwich and my laugh threatens to spill out as she slowly brings it to her mouth with a scared expression.

"That you'd learn Korean before coming."

She nibbles a bite. "Just between training." She chews and then swallows the breadcrumb she ate.

"What do you do anyway?" I ask. "Like for fun."

The sandwich sits in her lap and she stares out at the street like it holds the answer I'm asking for.

She shrugs. "The usual, go out with my friends, movies, bars. Probably the same things you do."

"I doubt that." I ball up my first sandwich wrapper and shoot it into the nearby trashcan. "Three points." I murmur.

I unwrap my second sandwich and I take a big bite.

"Why do guys do that? Have to shoot a basket every time they throw something away?"

I laugh, chewing and looking down at her. "Because it's fun," I mumble, covering my mouth.

She brings the sandwich back up to her lips and I wait for her to take a second bird bite. "I'll have to take your word for it." This time she takes a normal sized bite.

"No, you don't." I offer my hand, crunching the second sandwich wrapper into a ball.

She accepts my hand with her free one.

"Here." I place the wrapper in her hand.

"This is ridiculous."

"Humor me." I eye the wad of paper.

She takes another bite of her sandwich and then throws the paper and it hits the side of the trashcan. "See, stupid."

"You're just upset that you didn't score a point." I jog over and get the wrapper from the ground to bring it back. I take a seat beside her and hold out my hand.

She doesn't hold out her hand this time but rather stares at mine. "It was on the street."

"Yeah, it was. We'll sanitize your hands after." I look down at her purse. "I'm sure you have a bottle or two."

She scoffs and hip checks me. Good, we're back to touching.

I hold the paper in the air to drop it and she finally puts her hand out.

"Try to arch it more." I imitate a basketball throw.

She purses her lips, handing her sandwich to me.

"The competitor is coming out now."

She ignores me, crunching the paper in both of her hands. Her tongue licks her bottom lip and she throws it. She's got a good arc and it goes into the trashcan.

"Impressive."

She acts like she's waving off my compliments, but I see her smile. Then she opens up her purse and grabs a small bottle of sanitizer.

I stand there, holding her sandwiches. She looks over at me with those gorgeous green eyes of hers. I don't mention that I was right about the sanitizer. Then she grabs her sandwich, finishes eating it, crumples up the paper and throws it again into the trashcan. A perfect three points.

"Addictive, huh?"

She shrugs, and I hand her the last sandwich.

"Nah, you can have it."

"Split it?" I offer, tearing it in half.

"Sure."

I not only taught her how to throw a three-pointer into a trashcan, but proved to her that street food isn't that bad. My skills and experiences might be different than hers, but it feels nice to show her a new thing or two.

Outside of the bedroom that is.

CHAPTER ELEVEN

Demi and I stare up at the ride. A giant circle sways back and forth the entire length of the park and out over the river. My phone dings in my pocket. I hit ignore without looking at the name.

"You can take it," Demi says, spooning a frozen sorbet thing we just bought.

"Nah."

"Okay, let's go before I second guess this." She starts walking toward the entrance.

"You race down a hill at eighty miles per hour, but you can't ride a simple amusement park ride?"

Her attention is fixated on the motion of the ride, her head moving side to side. "I've been doing that since I was five."

"Seriously? You don't get out much, do you?"

She throws away the sorbet, pulls out her sanitizer, squirts it on her hands and rubs it all over her palms. "My mom keeps me busy."

I have a feeling there's more to this mom thing then she's saying, but I'm not going to pry. If I pry then I care, and if I care then we're more than just short-lived hookup buddies.

My phone dings again and I pick it up to mute it when the picture on the screen stops me.

"Fucking hell," I mumble.

"What?" she asks, pretending not to peer over my shoulder.

I turn my phone her way and her mouth drops open. Her head twists around searching for the culprit.

The picture is of us, her kissing my cheek as she takes the sorbet from my hands while I'm paying the vendor. It came from Beckett, which means he's around here somewhere, with Skylar no doubt.

"I wonder where they are?" she asks.

"Who cares. Let's ride." The line opens up and she accepts my decision to just ride and forget them. Maybe we can meet up with them later.

We take our seats, the harness comes down and we buckle in. Her chest heaves like it usually does after we're done banging, so I reach over and grab her hand.

"This is safe, right?" she asks.

I laugh. "Completely."

She nods a few times, her eyes cast down. Then she lifts her chin, her head pressed against the back of the ride, her eyes shut tight.

The ride starts swaying a few times, gradually getting higher and higher. Demi's eyes are still shut, little groans coming from her as we drop and head to the next side. I hold her hand in mine while her other free hand clutches the metal bar.

"We're almost done," I say, and she peeks one eye open and shuts it again quickly.

"Liar."

"One glimpse," I urge her right as we're over the river.

She opens her eyes, but we fall down to the other side and since we're on top now, our bodies feel the pull of gravity.

"Fuck! How did you convince me to do this?" Her eyes shut and she lets go of my hand, gripping the other metal handle for dear life.

I laugh.

"It's not funny. We're going to die. I'm going to die before I even have a chance to compete."

I laugh harder this time and her foot moves to the side to kick me.

"Maybe you just need to be distracted," I say. "Should I take of my coat and shirt?"

She huffs and I know if her eyes were open she'd be rolling them and I smile.

"Not even the sight of your Sochi tattoo on those pecs of yours can help me now."

I chuckle.

"Speaking of, you didn't have that tattoo when we were fooling around four years ago."

"I got it after the games. I'll get one after these games, too. Something to remember them by."

"Makes sense," she says.

I'm thinking I may have successfully distracted her when the ride jolts a bit and she let's a cry out and grips even tighter.

"Okay, okay, relax. We're slowing down now. Almost done."

The tension in her body diminishes the tiniest bit. If I wasn't so in tune with her body, I probably wouldn't have noticed.

"Thank God."

The ride comes to an end a few seconds later and Demi can't get out of the harness fast enough.

"Okay, that was my one adrenaline rush today." She points her finger at me.

I grab her finger and pull her to me, my lips landing on hers. She doesn't fight me or push me away. She wraps her arms around my waist, inching up on her toes to get even closer to me.

"I'm proud of you," I say, once I pull back.

A smile I've yet to see crosses her lips. It almost makes me think she doesn't hear that nearly enough.

"Thanks." She rises on her toes one more time, planting a kiss on my lips. "Can we shop now?"

I roll my eyes. "Sure."

Hand in hand we leave the ride, but my phone dings again and I don't even have to look to see who it's from because four sets of eyes are focused on us when we step out of the exit.

———

"FUNNY MEETING YOU HERE," Grady says, fist bumping me.

Mia swarms Demi and a reluctant Skylar joins the girls in what is probably a mission ditch Dax conversation.

"Funny, asshole," I say to Beckett whose two dimples are so far indented into his face that I'd like to punch the smug look right off.

"Hey, you gave me the ammo," he holds his hands out to his sides.

"How was the game show?" Grady asks, wrapping his arm around Mia now that the girls' private convo is over.

We share a look and shrug. "Kind of a letdown," Demi answers.

"Well, we're heading to some Bar-B-Que place." Beckett thumbs away from where we're at. "Wanna join?"

"Sure," Demi says way too fast for my liking.

I would've been happy to spend the day with just her, but my friends are cool, too. I just can't touch her as much with them here. That's the suck ass part.

We walk to the restaurant as a group. Grady and Mia are all touchy-feely, Skylar's arm is now linked through Demi's, leaving me with Beckett, who won't stop side glancing me.

"What?" I ask.

He shrugs. "Nothing."

We leave Lotte World, the amusement park, and I keep waiting for Skylar to stop her rambling about what they all did this morning and what train did we take, and can Demi believe how fast it was. My body hums for Demi to walk closer to me. To watch her put on her lip balm, to point things out or to share a laugh when someone really odd walks by. I don't want to walk with Beckett. I mean he's cool and everything but if I had a choice...

"I'm surprised you stayed in Seoul. Don't you have to get back?" Beckett asks.

He's right. My prelims are in two days. The last thing I should be doing is walking the streets of Seoul, eating their food, but lately, the Classics are the furthest thing from my mind. I'd have my thumb up my ass if I stayed back anyway. I did my workout and my visualization exercises this morning, so in my books, I'm good.

"It's just a waiting game until qualifiers. Figured some down time might do me good."

He slaps me on the back. "We'll be there for you, brah."

The California accent that earned him the nickname Hoff appears briefly.

"Thanks."

"And I'm sure Demi will be there, too."

I look at him from the corner of my eye. "Stop digging. We're just having fun."

He nods and says nothing else, but I know his mind is working overtime. It always is.

Ten minutes later we walk into the restaurant and I'm hoping I can arrange it so I can sit next to Demi. Surely a little touchy feely on the upper thigh is okay.

But Skylar being the cockblocker she's become, somehow manipulates the entire situation so that Demi and I are seated across from each other. I can't even play footsie with her since the table has a grill in the middle of it.

She looks over at me, smiling and then placing the napkin in her lap and picking up her menu. Guess she doesn't really care.

The waitress comes over, and we pretty much order whatever she suggests since we can't understand the menu. Although we've had Korean Bar-B-Que when we came for the press tour, others took care of our ordering for us because of the language barrier.

Then it was like a buffet was set up on our table. Bowls with small portions came out filled with cucumbers, radishes, bean sprouts and a bunch of other ones with sauce over them, soup, salad, white rice. The traditional kimchi placed down.

"Sake?" the waitress asks, holding a small bottle up in the air with six shot glasses on her tray.

"Definitely." Beckett raises his hand.

Says the man that's done competing. Demi and I both

decline since we're only days away now, but the other four don't mind sharing the bottle.

The waitress brings a tray of meat and picks up the items, putting the pieces on the grill in the middle of the table.

"This is so fun" Demi says, sitting up a little straighter in her chair.

She takes her chopsticks, and looks to the bowls, picking up a piece of cucumber and eating it. Her movements are so flawless, while I'm just thankful the waitress brought us forks and spoons. They must be used to the foreigners with the Classics going on.

"Want to learn?" Demi asks me since my eyes are fixated on her placing the cucumber in her mouth.

It's not the chopsticks I want right now but I'll play along.

"My hands are way too big to handle those."

She laughs and all four of our friend's heads twist her way. Demi raises her eyebrows staring back at them like what's the matter?

"You laughed?" Mia asks.

"Yeah, people tend to do that when I speak," I say.

Demi laughs again, rolling her eyes.

"She did it again?" Skylar says.

"I'm not a robot, guys. I do have a sense of humor." Demi places the chopsticks down and a pink flush washes over her pale face and neck.

"But it was Dax. You laughed at Dax." Mia literally sounds confused by the situation.

Demi's gaze rests on me. "He's kind of funny." The look on her face says it's more like we have a private joke that we really don't want to share with others.

"I'm so confused. I thought you guys were just fucking," Skylar chimes in.

"We are," Demi confirms and then looks to me, eyes wide like she needs me to back her up.

"Yeah, we're in it strictly for the orgasms."

Demi laughs again, and the girls share a look amongst themselves, but let it rest.

"Now do you want me to show you?" Demi asks, already getting out of her seat to come over.

"You can show me anything. Preferably your tits." I lean back in my seat.

She smacks me upside the back of my head.

"There you go. Now we're back to normal," Beckett comments as the four of them ding their shot glasses in a toast and sip their sake.

I'm starting to wonder if there's no going back to normal for Demi and me.

CHAPTER TWELVE

The one good thing about Demi and I still having our events is that we hop on a train back to the village by ourselves while the other four stay to go to a club. There were days I'd go to that club and get shit-faced whether I had to train the next day or not. But today, alone time with her sounds like a better option.

She walks the train and although I love watching her ass, I'm ready to sit the fuck down and relax. Maybe even take a nap on the way back. I ate way too much food, but the amount of walking we did today should've counteracted it. At least, I hope.

Finally, she slides into a bench seat and I slide in the one across from her so we can face each other. I prop my feet up on the empty space next to her and rest my head back.

"Tired?" she asks.

"Eh." I shrug my shoulders watching out the window, waiting for the train to start.

It's late enough that most everyone's commute is over, but early enough people are still out partying, so the entire station and train almost seem deserted. Which will be beneficial for my nap. I close my eyes and let out a long breath.

"You know we can't fall asleep, right?" She kicks me with her foot.

It seems like ages ago that she last showed me any of her aggressive affection.

"Why would that be?" I pry one eye open.

"Robbers," she says it like I'm an idiot for not knowing. "When I was a senior in high school, we went to Europe for a class trip and my friend got all her money and her passport stolen."

"Because she fell asleep on a train?"

"Yep."

"So, we're not sleeping on the train?" I ask for clarification although I'm certain of the answer.

"Nope."

I move my feet down to the floor, sit up a little straighter. "We should've grabbed some coffee before we got on."

She's staring at me like she's waiting for me to say something.

"What?"

She leans forward, her hands sliding up my jeans, her thumbs on the inside of my thighs and she casually gets up and kisses me on the lips while her hand presses down on my crotch.

Maybe I'm not as tired as I thought.

"Maybe we could do other things to stay awake?" she whispers in my ear and then falls back to her seat.

"Why so far away?" I pat the spot next to me.

She pats the spot next to her.

Hell, I don't have to win this round. I get up, shrug off my jacket and sit down next to her.

I lean into her neck like I'm giving her a kiss. "Unzip your coat," I say in her ear.

Her fingers move to the zipper, and I wait to see those tits my hands have missed all day.

"Put it over your lap," I say once she's worked her coat free.

She does as directed, and I place mine over my lap, like they're blankets we're using for warmth.

The train pulls away from the station, the city lights fading, darkening the sky, which effectively darkens the train since the lights are lowered for the people who want to sleep like I did seconds before Demi restored my energy with her genius idea.

"Lean back and close your eyes," I say.

I'm not sure what the rules for public indecency are in Korea, but I don't really want to find out, so I figure we can pretend to sleep.

Instead of her head falling back or toward the window, she presses her face into the side of my arm.

My fingers walk up a path over her hipbone and up to the waist of her leggings. Thank God for leggings and their easy access.

Her arms wrap around mine, tightening as I slowly tuck my hand under the waistband, but just enough to tease her. I go over the top of her panties. Panties that are already wet, but not nearly as soaked as I would've liked. My finger glides along the lace trim, feeling the smooth skin underneath.

Grabbing her panties, I pull them up slowly, and they slide into her folds rubbing against her clit. She loves anything that involves her clit and she comes quickly when I concentrate my efforts there, so I let go, my finger traveling down the front of her panties once more.

She groans into my arm, her teeth scraping my bicep.

My palm presses down on her clit with enough pressure that she squeals. Her wetness coats my fingers and I slide her panties aside, my pointer and ring finger teasing her opening.

Her hands grip tighter on my arm as if she's willing me not to stop. Does she not know me at all? We go all the way, every time.

I slide my palm back up and my fingers graze under her panties when the door of the train opens, and a conductor walks through.

Great timing.

He stops a man who looks half asleep and starts chatting in Korean. His gaze flicks to us momentarily and I smile while my hand continues its path of exploration.

I spread my fingers, positioning her clit between my pointer and middle finger. Squeezing it gently but firm enough that it doesn't slip, my palm puts more pressure on her mound, the tips of my fingers running up and down the slick folds.

Again, her teeth latch on to my skin and her ass slides on the bench, her legs widening.

My mouth waters, wanting to taste her and have her come on my tongue instead of on my fingers. Not that she's enjoying it any less.

Out of the corner of my eye, I see the conductor say goodbye to the other guy and he heads our way. We nod, and he looks at our tickets placed on the metal prongs, clicking his puncher on them.

Not stopping my hand under the jackets, his vision never even goes there until Demi groans.

He backs up one step, looking from her to me.

"A dream. Crossing my fingers it's about me." I hold up my free hand with crossed fingers.

The scowl doesn't leave his face and I'm not even sure if he understood me.

He scrutinizes the situation once more and then carries on, right as I use the magic touch and Demi coats my entire hand.

She lifts her head and rests it on my arm, staring up at me like I'm a rock star and damn if I couldn't get used to looking at that face every day.

I'm starting to realize that I might just be fucked. And not in the literal sense.

CHAPTER THIRTEEN

I 've always hated Valentine's Day. Ever since I was younger, before it was mandatory that every kid gives every other kid in class a valentine. Not that my box was ever empty, but I stressed the entire night before about whether a girl would drop one in my box.

Grady and Mia stayed in Seoul to celebrate and Beckett and Skylar were hanging out with her family.

After my morning workout I headed to the local stores and now I'm knocking on the familiar door of Demi Harrison.

"Hey you." She swings the door wide open and heads back to the desk where she continues putting on her makeup.

I hold up the two bags in my hand. "Happy Valentine's Day."

Her mouth hangs open, surprise etched in every one of her features. "I didn't get you anything."

I take a seat and pat the spot next to me on the bed. She stands, a frown forming on her face the closer she gets to me.

"Relax. It's not a diamond necklace."

She sits down. "Well, break my heart why don't you." The grin on her face says she's not serious.

Why would she be? The words about how she expects nothing from me keep rattling around in my head. Something I'm not used to.

"Bag one." I hold out the red gift bag with no tissue paper and nothing to make it seem even remotely special by any means. I keep telling myself I don't want her to make a big deal about it.

She sets it on her lap, glancing my way before opening it.

"Oh my God, I'm going to have to hide these." She pulls out a bunch of candy bars, suckers, and chips. She leans over and kisses me on the cheek. "Thank you."

"That was for drawer number one. Now for drawer number two." I hand her the pink bag. The one that took me a while to find, but luckily Koreans are as horny as the rest of the world apparently.

Her smile widens, but she appears hesitant to open it. She peeks in and then shuts it, looking at me from the corner of her eye.

"Don't act shy." I chuckle.

She slowly opens the bag and her hands take out each item. "A cock ring, handcuffs, a blindfold, and a feather."

"I didn't know how freaky you'd get, so I kept it conservative. I figured you didn't have much in drawer number two as far as sex toys you can use with someone else."

She sets the bag on the bed next to the array of toys. "Why do you assume that?"

Her face is straight-laced and I think I offended her. "Well—"

"Do you think I'm a prude?"

"No, I—"

"That I'd never do anything but missionary? I think I've proven to you, my experience isn't limited."

"Well, yeah, wait." I raise my hand. "What are we talking about here? Like the number of partners you've had? Or have you had the lesbo experience? Tell me all about it."

Images flash through my mind and, oh hell yeah, if we're talking lesbo shit I wanna know all about it.

She pushes me on the chest and I collapse to her pillow. Crawling up my body, she swings a leg on either side of me.

"You want to hear about me and Skylar? How before you came, we'd share that small bed over there?" Her hands are planted on my chest, my hands molded to her hips.

"Anyone but Skylar and I'd be all game," I deadpan.

"Mia?" she asks.

"Shit. No. Someone else."

She laughs falling on top of me, her hand running along my cheek in the most affectionate way anyone has ever done causing shivers to race over my skin.

I roll us over.

"Ouch." She squirms, and I pick up my head to look at her.

"I know I'm rock solid, but you've never complained before?"

She shakes her head, a smile teasing her lips. "I fell this morning."

"Where?" I sit up, my eyes scouring her body like I have x-ray vision and can see through her clothes.

"My hip, but I'm fine." She waves me off, but my hands unbutton her jeans, pulling them down.

"I'm fine, really."

"Lift your ass."

She does.

"Dax, it's nothing that I haven't dealt with before."

I get her jeans to mid-thigh, and she rolls over. Sure enough, there's a huge bruise on her left hip and ass.

"Shit, Demi," My hand hesitantly runs over her injury.

"Remember this next time you think I'm chicken for not wanting to go on a rollercoaster."

She laughs it off, but I don't find it very funny. It's all black and blue and will definitely affect her upcoming performance in the Classics.

"Demi, it's bad. Did your mom see it, the trainers?"

She nods, sucks in a breath and her eyes are glass so I know she's fighting tears. I just don't know if it's the pain from the injury or something else. "It's the cost of competing at this level. You know that as well as I do. Now."

She holds out her arms, but I can't in good faith hand-cuff her to the bed like I planned. I had visions of being more on the rough side, but she's already dealt with enough today.

I shake my head getting up from the bed and walk into the bathroom.

"Dax," she sighs.

I come back out of the bathroom, grabbing her jacket off the hanger on the back of the door. "Pull up your pants."

Her back is resting on her headboard. "That's not something I ever thought I'd hear you say."

"Trust me, me either, but we're going to my room."

Rising to her feet, she buttons her jeans.

"And grab a pair of sweatpants."

"Sweatpants and Valentine's Day don't really mix."

"You underestimate yourself. You can make sweatpants sexy." I waggle my eyebrows.

She stops all movement, her eyes on me, a smile on her lips. "Did you just compliment me?"

I grab her hand, placing her jacket in it. "You act like I never say nice things to you."

"Well..."

I shake my head, we're not going to start a fight when she needs to get some damn ice on that injury.

"What about the bag?" she asks once we're half out the door.

I head back in the room, grab bag number one and join her at the door.

"I was thinking bag number two," she says in a low voice that almost has me turning around to grab it off the bed.

"Are you crazy? There's no sex play tonight." I grab her hand and we start walking down the hall after she locks her door.

"What fun is that? I want to use all the toys you bought."

A group of guys looks at us as I'm dragging her down the hall.

"Let her use the toys, man," one dipshit shouts once he's a good distance away.

"Mind your own fucking business," I yell back.

The group laugh and head down the stairway.

After a few minutes, we reach the door to my room.

"This seems so unnecessary," she says. "I get bruises all the time."

I dig into my jacket for the keys. "Yeah, but you probably didn't have your prelims so soon after."

She saddles up to me, her fingers raking down the front of my shirt and then she twists her hand and palms my dick through my pants. "I don't want you to take it easy tonight."

"Good thing it's not your choice." I open my door. "Now it's not all pretty and nice like yours, but it has what we need."

She steps into my personal space, her eyes taking in the empty walls, the half-made bed, the clothes thrown over the desk chair.

"I said no judging." I head to the bathroom to grab the ace bandage and towels.

"It's very minimalistic."

"Is that a nice way to say ugly?" I ask.

She's sitting on my bed when I get out and I head to the mini fridge and freezer, grabbing a couple of ice packs.

"No. I'm just surprised you have nothing personal here."

She eyes Grady's side of the room where there's a neatly made bed, although I guarantee that was Mia. But he does have pictures of his family, all of his shit lined up nicely, whereas my deodorant and hair gel are strewn across my dresser along with spare change and anything else I dig out of my pockets at night.

"We're here for only a few weeks." I shrug then wave my hand in the air for her to stand.

She obliges, but her eyes are still scrutinizing where I sleep.

My hands move to the button of her jeans, and then the zipper. Her lids grow heavy as she watches. I pull them down to the floor and she steps out of them, her fingers now threading through my hair for balance.

Being eye level with her pussy and seeing the wet spot on her panties, doesn't exactly make it easy to do the right thing. But more than I want to get laid right now, I want to do the right thing by Demi and I'm choosing to ignore why that might be the case.

I lean forward, inhaling her scent and placing my lips on the wet silk of her panties. Her hands tighten in my hair and for a second, I consider ripping the fabric from her body.

"I'm going to miss you tonight," I say.

She giggles, and I rise to my feet, kissing her lips.

"You're cockblocking yourself?"

Needing just one more taste of her, I grip the back of her neck and pull her to me. She yelps but the surprise quickly falls away as she meets the frantic pace of my kiss.

I pull away abruptly. "Okay, focus, Dax," I say to myself. "Lay down on your side." I nod at the bed behind her.

"Hmm...that sounds promising."

She lays down on my bed in my sheets and I chastise myself mentally for how much I seem to like that. Demi flinches when I press the towel covered ice pack over her bruise. I've been where she is, and I know it sucks balls, but she's got to heal a bit before her event.

Wrapping the ace bandage around her leg, my fingers graze her panties more than once and my poor, frustrated dick twitches each and every time. She's not helping—each time my fingers brush against the silk a small moan escapes her. I have to blink to make my eyes focus on my goal.

After she's all set, I put a pillow under her thigh and hand her the remote. "You need to sit there twenty minutes with the ice."

She takes the remote, resting it in her hand.

I turn to step away, but her hand grips mine. "Dax."

Her voice is so soft I can barely hear her, but I turn back around.

"Thank you."

I swear her eyes look watery, but why would they be? All I did was wrap her leg and refuse to have sex with her.

"We're friends, right?" I ask, re-establishing the boundaries we put in place.

Her lips dip slightly before she smiles. "Yeah. Friends."

I swallow down the lump in my throat and go to my fridge, grabbing us some electrolyte fruit drinks. Maybe I should have just slept with her. Seems like it would've been easier.

CHAPTER FOURTEEN

O ur heads rest millimeters apart, our fingers inches away from one another, our breaths releasing in an even stream. With my laptop propped up on my suitcase, we Netflix and Chill in the literal sense.

"Hey, can I ask you a question?" I turn toward her.

"What?" Her eyes remain on the screen.

"Do you love alpine skiing?"

She doesn't respond right away. She winces, turning her body sideways to look at me.

"Don't."

She shakes off my concern. "I'm good." Her hands tuck under my pillow and there's something way too intimate going on right now, but this must be what having a girl for a friend is like.

I've never had a real female friend before and that's half the reason I don't understand Beckett and Skylar. They're always touching each other without ever getting to the really good stuff. What's the point? But having Demi in my bed warms parts of me that are normally cold and vacant.

Being friends with a girl is a lot different than being one with a guy.

"I'll answer the question if you answer one of mine," she finally says.

Of course, I should've known Demi wouldn't put herself out there if I wasn't prepared to do the same. The question is, am I? Not many people in my life know about my family situation. Grady and Brandon are the only ones. All Beckett really knows is my family is as absent as his.

"Okay, but be kind," I say.

She giggles, her hand shoving me. "Sure."

She thinks for a moment, her eyes staring up at the ceiling and she inhales a few deep breaths. "I did. I mean, I do enjoy it." Her face scrunches. "I think I'd like it a lot more if my mom wasn't so involved. She makes it hard. It's the classic story of a child never feeling good enough."

I nod. From the small things she's mentioned I figured as much. "Why don't you ask her to stop coaching you?"

She huffs. "Have you met my mother?"

"I haven't had the pleasure."

"She'd never let me train solely with another coach where she didn't have any input. Mother knows best. She's a three-time medalist. Her not being involved is not even a remote possibility." The smile on her face looks forced and I hate it. "It's not all bad though. I mean I might not be here if it wasn't for her. She pushed me when I wanted to play with Barbies instead. And I do have love for the sport. When I'm on that hill, she's not in my ear and it's just me and my skis. Those are my favorite moments."

"What would you do if you didn't ski?"

It's a tough question and I don't even have an answer if I was asked myself. During off-season, I freak out about what I'll do when I'm too old to compete in this sport.

A long stream of breath leaves her mouth. "Teach it?" she laughs. "I have no idea. Every winter I've skied. My mom always arranged for me to go to school through summer to have the winters off. I know nothing else."

"Me either."

We sit in a comfortable silence for a minute before she speaks again.

"Is it my turn now? You asked two."

I chuckle, always one to stay on course. "Hit me."

"Your family, how come they don't come to support you?"

"Man, you're hitting the bullseye first." I lay my hand over my heart, implying this is the topic I don't really like to talk about. Which is putting it mildly.

"Hey, you hit me where it hurt, too."

I shake my head because she's got me there. "Ah, my family. I could say finances. My mom always says she has to work. My brothers both have families."

"But you're competing to be the best in the world. It doesn't get any bigger than that."

This is why I never talk to people about it. It's hard for them to understand.

"I've offered to pay, but they say they can watch it on television. That the money should go to something better than traveling and staying in a hotel."

Her lips turn down and her forehead crinkles.

Yeah, I don't get it either.

"What does your mom do?"

"She's a waitress."

That does nothing to change her look. Nope, she's not some high-power attorney who can't get a moment of free time for herself. She's not a doctor on call. She serves drinks at a rundown bar in the middle of Vermont.

"I don't know, I'm the youngest and my mom was so busy working to put food on the table that there wasn't much time or attention left for me."

"What about your dad?"

"Nu-uh. My turn."

She smiles that million-dollar grin I'm starting to become addicted to.

"Julien? Did you, do you love him?"

I'm not sure why I care, but when I saw her face at the karaoke night and how hurt she was, I wondered if there was more to it than just dating.

"God, no." She rolls onto her back, entwining her hands over her stomach, her chest rising up and falling with deep breaths. Then she turns back my way, but her eyes shift around like she doesn't want to look directly at me. "I think it was like the last straw, but more like the last guy."

"Meaning?"

She tilts her head as though I'm supposed to get what she's saying.

"It was four years ago for us," I say.

"True...but since then I haven't had a true relationship. All the guys I date seem to like me enough to sleep with me, but that's about it. I mean, I get that we all have crazy schedules and it's hard to get something started, but it's like I wasn't worth it. Being tossed aside—again—it hurts." A tear slips down her cheek.

Fuck. My heart hiccups, my stomach clenches so hard I swallow down the bile rising from the disgust I feel at being one of the guys who made her feel that way.

"I'm sorry." I hope she can hear the sincerity in my voice.

"Don't be. It's just..." She pauses, and I let her collect her thoughts rather than interrupting like I usually do in uncomfortable situations. "It probably all stems from my relationship with my mom. I'm sure a counselor would have a field day with my mommy issues. It's like I'll never be good enough in her eyes and I think I find that feeling easy to transfer over to other relationships."

Makes sense and it doesn't surprise me that she knows this about herself. One thing about Demi is that she's not a bullshitter. Not with anyone else and apparently not with herself either.

"That's why I agreed to this thing between us. I needed to have some fun and know that there were no expectations. So, thank you." Her hand nudges my shoulder. "I've had a lot of fun this Winter Classics."

Again, the fact that she has no expectations of me gnaws at my gut when it should make me rejoice.

"So...your dad?" she asks, switching topics.

I huff. "Your guess is as good as mine. He walked out when I was one and never returned."

She blows out a long breath. "Oh, that sucks."

"Not really. If he doesn't want to be part of my life, then I don't want to be part of his."

I've always been fine with the fact my dad left. My brothers feel differently but maybe that's because they remember him more. You can't miss something you never had. There were times I'd see Grady and his dad or Brandon and his, and think what if, but I've been on my own for so long that I accept it for what it is.

"That's very untherapeutic. A counselor wouldn't make any money off of you." She giggles.

"I'm sure if you dug deep enough you could find something worth exploring."

She slides closer to me, her hand cradling my cheek. "I bet that's true. You're nothing like what I assumed."

I knock my forehead with hers. "Is that a compliment?"

"Yeah, it is."

A spurt of electric energy erupts in my stomach and I suck in a breath because whatever it was, it felt good...too fucking good.

"Your turn," she whispers. I want to feel her body, but I know the best thing for her is rest, so I try to use all that willpower I have and keep my hands to myself.

"Favorite color?"

She draws her head back, studying my face. "Aqua. You?"

"Black."

"Heartless, huh?"

"I was kidding, Manatee."

"Manatee? What color is that?"

I shake my head like I'm disappointed in her. "Have you never read the colors on crayons?"

"No. Typically I stick with the color wheel." She chuckles.

"You're missing out then. Manatee is a grayish blue. And there's not just Aquamarine, there's Caribbean Green or Tropical Rain Forest. You really need to up your game if we're going to be friends."

I stiffen my body in anticipation of a playful hit. Usually, when I say some smart-ass remark, her reflex is to hit or kick me. Instead, her lips land on mine, her hand holding me in place by the back of my neck.

Our tongues instantly perfect the dance they've been practicing the past week and soon I'm on my back with her on top of me.

She slows the kiss. "You're an odd duck, Dax Campbell."

"You love that about me, admit it."

I feel her smile against my lips. "Yeah, I do."

I ease her off my body. "Stop trying to take advantage of me. You need to ice again."

She falls to her back, her eyes rolling as she does. "The best remedy would be sex."

I roll off the bed and head over to the freezer. "You really are insatiable."

She shrugs.

"I must be killer in bed."

She throws a towel across the room at me. "Cocky ass."

"It's not cocky if it's the truth." I signal for her to roll over and she does as I ask, and I place the ice pack on her bruise. "No worries, babe, once this is better, I plan on making up for lost time."

"I'm holding you to that."

Finally, she expects something from me.

CHAPTER FIFTEEN

"You ready? This is it." Coach Fitzgerald slaps me on my back and I fumble forward.

I can already feel how off I am. Demi and I stayed up late, talking about how drastically different our childhoods were. She grew up near Aspen in what I imagine is a mansion on a mountain. Whereas I, scraped change up off the sidewalk just to buy a candy bar on the way home from school. Her bedroom held a canopy bed and mine a twin mattress on the floor in the corner of a bedroom I shared with my brothers.

I didn't tell Demi everything, I didn't want to appear like I was that lacking, but I think she got the point when I mentioned how I loved to go over to Grady's house growing up because there was always drinks and snacks out for their B&B guests. We were poor, but I survived.

Maybe if I would've been handed everything I wanted I wouldn't have strived to be where I am now. I wouldn't be standing on top of this mountain questioning whether I can do enough to make it to the finals.

My body is drained, and it hasn't escaped me that I

didn't sleep with Demi last night which means all the luck is gone. What's wrong with me? Her leg sucks but not that bad, she could've had sex. She definitely *wanted* to have sex and like a moron, I turned her down. Now I'll be dragging ass all day.

The truth is I forgot all about the luck thing. I haven't even thought about it in days.

"Hey," a soft, feminine voice stops me before I get up to the starting gate to get ready.

Before I even have a chance to say hello, her lips press to mine, her mitten-covered hands on my cheeks. "Good luck," she says with the sincerest eyes I've ever encountered.

"Thanks. Someone kept me up last night."

She flutters her eyes. "At least you didn't expend any energy."

I lean in closer to make sure none of the other guys can hear me. "That changes tonight."

"Hey, you win gold and I'll be your celebratory prize."

My dick literally shoots up in my pants. "Done."

"You're next," Coach yells and then looks at who I'm talking to. "Oh, hey, Demi. When do you compete?"

They start talking about how it sucks being at the end of the Classics, then Coach asks about her mom and the light in her eyes diminishes a bit.

"So, you think our boy can do it?" Coach asks teasingly.

I sit down on the chair, clipping into my board and glance up. Our eyes lock and her attention is on me when she answers.

"I hope so, otherwise I'll be running for my life." She makes like she's feeling money between her thumb and index finger, as if she bet on me. "But it's his. I know it."

I mouth thank you then stand up on my board. "How about one more kiss?"

She glances at Coach and then jogs up to me. She raises to her tiptoes and lightly presses her lips to mine. A few of the guys lingering around whistle and sure enough as soon as she falls back on her heels, her cheeks are red and not from the wind this high up on the mountain.

"Don't fuck it up." She smacks me lightly in the stomach, turning and walking back down toward the spectator's area. Glancing over her shoulder, she smiles. "I'll meet you at the bottom."

I nod, watching her go. Hopefully, a kiss is enough to get me seeded well.

"Okay, Romeo, let's get set." Coach raises his eyebrows, no doubt wondering what's going on with me and Demi.

I place my goggles over my eyes, strap my mittens again, rock my hips a few times and then nod to Coach.

Minutes later, the metal gate slams down and I jet out onto the icy terrain. I hate riding by myself—I much prefer a challenger next to me. Maybe because the reason I compete so hard is that I've done it my entire life with my brothers. Always fighting for the remote, the last helping of food, Mom's attention.

My mind shifts back to last night with Demi and my heart speeds up knowing she's down there waiting for me, ready to give me a hug after my killer score goes up on that screen.

The line between Demi and me is blurring. I may have never been in a serious relationship my entire life, but I can still feel the energy shifting. It's no longer only sexually charged. There's a familiarity between us. A calmness inside me different from the storm that's usually brewing—the one that wants to go crazy jumping off of shit and pushing the limits, say whatever I want no matter who I offend.

The killer of all it is that I'm enjoying myself. Finding out about her, what she loves and what she hates last night was somehow fun. I didn't even care if we slept together. That might be a bit of a stretch, I am a testosterone-laden male after all, but the fact that we didn't have sex didn't diminish the night.

With all the mental thoughts traveling through my head, I realize I'm about to cross the finish line and I remember none of the race. Not one single turn, or jump, or whether I was able to keep my air low.

Shit, I probably strolled down the course like a grandma in the grocery aisle. I'm going to be seeded last and have to work my way up. *Fuck.*

I come to a stop, and the crowd is cheering so either they're cheering because they feel sorry for me, or I didn't do half bad. The screen takes forever to update, and I wait for the judges while I rack my brain trying to remember anything from the last few minutes.

My time goes up and the crowd cheers louder. I pump my fist in the air, unclipping myself from my board and walking through the opening in the inflatable barrier. Demi's arms wrap around my neck and her lips kiss my cheek before I can even talk to the press.

Guess our...friendship...is out there for all to see now.

A few cameras snap the picture.

"I knew you'd do it. Congratulations," she whispers in my ear, stepping back to give my other friends room to approach.

Grady, Beckett, and Brandon fist bump me and Mia and Skylar both say their congratulations.

One of the interviewers, Nik, a snowboarder in his own right pulls me aside. Nik retired after the last Classics and he's trying to make a name for himself as a reporter here.

"Dax, or Soups, that's what they call you, right?"

"Yeah," I say.

"How does it feel? You seemed to hit some kind of zone out there. You had a near flawless run like you were on autopilot."

"I guess, yeah."

"Man of few words, that's unusual for you. A lot of athletes have superstitions before they compete in something like this. You have any that helped you out on the course today?"

I glance back to my group of friends. Beckett's smug smile is the first thing I notice, but Demi's sweet grin with her hands pressed together in front of her mouth like she just ran her best time is what I can't stop looking at.

"A girl?" Nik asks, looking between Demi and me. "Never thought I'd see the day."

"No!" I blurt out. "I mean... I don't believe in superstitions." I regret the words immediately.

What's the harm in saying Demi is my lucky charm? Other than the fact that now she'll think that's the only reason I'm sticking around. She doesn't need to know why I originally sought her out—it would ruin everything. After her whole 'I'm never good enough' confession last night, that's the last thing I ever want her to know especially when it holds no weight anymore. Hopefully, Beckett kept his trap shut and didn't tell that panty shield, Skylar.

Nik laughs. "Okay, well, as of right now you're seeded in top spot, so good luck on the way to the semifinals."

"Thanks, Nik." He walks away, ready to interview the next guy who's going to come off the course.

"Way to go! Man, I still can't believe how much you were in the zone today." Grady pulls my head down into a headlock.

I wiggle out of his hold. "Yeah, I just…I don't even know what to say." Demi seems reluctant to come over to me now and I have to think that it has to do with the interview. But what could she be mad about? I didn't do anything but say I don't believe in superstitions. My response had nothing to do with us.

"We're headed to the restaurant, wanna join?" Beckett asks, and he has to know the answer is no. I have semifinals in a few hours.

"No, I'm going to hit the pillow for a bit." My eyes veer to Demi who's busy eyeballing the snow instead of looking at me.

"Good idea," Beckett says. "We'll be back before your next run."

I give my friends a fist bump, while Mia gives me a quick hug and Skylar mumbles congratulations again. Demi just gives me a small smile and bypasses me to follow the others.

I reach out and grab her arm, tugging her back to me. "You wanna stay with me?"

She blinks like it surprises her that I want her with me. "You sure?"

That's when I know that whatever it is between us, things aren't so carefree anymore.

"Definitely. Nap?"

She wraps her arms around my waist, inching up on her toes and kissing my neck. "Maybe we can expend a little energy before our nap?"

Maybe I'm wrong because my little nympho has come out to play and what I thought was going to be a conversation about how I hurt her, is now about getting it on which shows how on page she is with this. The relief I expected to feel at that isn't there.

"How's your hip?" I ask.

"I think it needs to be stretched out with some rocking," she says with a grin.

"Well," I turn us toward the village, "how can I say no to helping out a fellow athlete?"

CHAPTER SIXTEEN

M y fists clench the sheets as her lips travel down my abs, her tongue slides up my length, teasing the tip and makes a path to the base of my shaft. I remember four years ago and how good she was and how much I loved watching my cock slide in and out of her mouth.

All my worries at the bottom of the slope disappear into ether because we must be on the same page as to what we want out of this—sex.

Stop thinking.

Her mouth is completely around me now, her hand pumping my base, the sound of slurping mixed with her moans is all I hear.

I try to keep my hands fisted in the sheets, not wanting to direct her. I'd rather just let her do her thing because she does it so damn well. I open my legs, my hips bucking because it's so fucking hot having her mouth on me that it's impossible not to do *something*. I'm surprised and impressed that I've lasted this long.

"Fuck, I'm gonna come," I rasp out.

Demi stays in place, continuing what she's doing, her

hair cascading down either side of her face, tickling my thighs. I know Demi swallows—that's not something a guy is likely to forget—and I'm more than happy to oblige her wishes. She reaches down and cups my balls, playing with them and I shoot like a rocket into the back of her throat.

She smiles at me over my now deflating dick and licks her lips before starting to move back up to me.

"What about you?" I ask, rolling her over.

"Ouch," she says.

"Shit, I forgot." I run my hand over her bruise.

"It's okay." Her hands wrap around my neck. "I'm good. You need to nap." She puts her feet under the blankets, pulling the sheets up over us.

"Nap?"

"Yeah, that's what you wanted to do, right? You need to make sure you're ready to go." She grabs her phone from the nightstand, thumbing the screen and then clicks it off. "When we wake up we can go get something to eat and then you're on."

I pull her into my chest, my arm wrapped around her shoulders, my finger lazily gliding along her spine. "You're like a mother hen."

She kisses my neck and then my chest, patting my stomach. "Night, night."

Is this weird? I mean she's lying naked in my arms and we're going to sleep together. We've done this...never. But I suppose we did just fool around, so this isn't exactly crossing a line.

So, I shut my eyes and go with it. It was *her* plan after all.

"GOOD LUCK." She kisses me on the lips at the top of the hill. "Not that you need it."

I sit in the chair, clipping into my board and adjusting my mittens.

"See you at the bottom," I say with a smile.

"I'll be waiting."

She touches Coach Fitzgerald's arm and then I watch her head down. She better hurry, otherwise I'll beat her.

"So, you and Demi, huh?" Coach asks then chuckles a bit. "Her mom is not going to like you."

I want to ask Coach a million questions about Demi's mom. Why won't she like me? Why is she so tough on Demi? But all the racers have just been called to the start gates.

"Red?" The guy who's in charge of putting us in stalls like we're a bunch of thoroughbreds calls out.

"Here." I raise my hand.

"First pick." He points to the starting gates.

I select the first gate. Since I had the best time on my first run, I pick first. I point to where I want. "Thanks."

"Don't think too hard," Coach says behind me and I turn to look at him like what the hell do you expect me to do here. "Well, you know what to do."

I nod, he's right, I do. Not that I don't love my coach, but at this point I just have to do what they taught me, trust that I'm ready. Years of hard work culminate into a few minutes on this mountainside.

I place my hands on the handles, sliding my board like I usually do, flexing my hips because that's what'll get me out ahead of the rest of the guys.

The metal gates come down and all six of us push off and head toward the first dip. The snow crunches under my board, the sun shines down on the track, making it a bit slushier than it was this morning. I'm keeping my air low and my speed high, but there's still a couple guys lingering around me.

I was meant for the race—the speed and the twists and turns. I love the competition. To know that when you're the first over the line, you're number one.

I shift my body low to the ground and then back up catching air. The bottom is coming up fast, only one more big hill and I'll be finished with this run.

Soon, I'm in the lead, which means I should be fine to secure a spot in the top three. A second later, I'm the first over the line and carving out my stop.

I glance over at the crowd, but I don't see Demi. I fist bump some of the other riders, then pull my goggles up, scouring the sidelines. She's not there.

Maybe she got distracted or didn't make it down the hill fast enough. All the riders start leaving the area to move out of the way for the next set of riders coming down. Once I'm through the exit, Nik is there, waiting with his microphone.

Grady, Mia, Beckett, and Skylar are all there, too, but still no Demi. Where the fuck did she go? She said she'd be at the bottom waiting.

I fist bump the guys. I may not understand much about women, but Mia and Skylar share a look that tells me something is up.

"Dax, looks like today is your day," Nik says, putting the microphone in my face.

"Yeah, I've been lucky."

"Maybe a lucky charm?"

My eyes flash to Beckett, but he slowly shakes his head and I wonder where the hell Nik came up with that on his own. Maybe I'm just stressed because Demi's not here. Why isn't she here?

"Just skill, Nik." I wink and clap him on the shoulder.

"Well, good luck on your upcoming races," Nik as I make to walk away.

"Thanks."

He drops the microphone, fist bumps me and then heads through the crowd. I have to admit he's doing a great job.

"Hey guys." I take off my helmet and rub my sweaty head with my gloved hand.

"Brandon will be here for the next one. He had an interview," Grady says, and I nod, though he's not the person I want to hear about. I mean I love Brandon and all, but he's not the one I've been sleeping with this whole time.

I look to Mia, hoping she'll tell me where Demi is. I'd prefer not to hear it from Skylar since she's so anti-Dax and Demi.

"Her mom texted her," Mia says and reaches out to me. "But she said she'll be back for the next one."

I nod and notice a guy on a snowmobile waiting to take me back up the hill.

"Okay, I'll see you guys."

"You got this," Beckett shouts right before the snowmobile roars to life and races away.

The competition is becoming even more fierce but as long as I land in the top three I'm in finals.

My mind is a jumbled mess on my next run. I manage to secure a spot, but I came in fucking third. Damn it, I won't be able to pick my lane. Hell, I'll probably be last this time.

Walking out of the inflatable exit isn't so great when Nik doesn't care to interview you. He's on to the bigger and better athletes who crossed the finish line first.

I fist bump the guys. Mia hugs me, whispering in my

ear. "She'll be here for your final, I know it." Good 'ol Mia, always the optimist.

I nod, but I can't help the gnawing feeling in my stomach. Like I'm missing something. Demi really must've been my lucky charm because she doesn't come to one race and I shit the bed.

I hop on the snowmobile again and let it take me up. I'd rather hang around up top awaiting my next run then down there where Demi's absence feels like a gaping hole.

Sure enough, I'm stuck with picking my stall third. Sucks ass.

I'm clipping into my board when I hear one of the volunteers call out. "Miss! You can't be here."

"Please, I'm a skier, see." It's Demi and I laugh at the thought of her showing her badge.

"Maybe you should find a skiing event then," the guy says.

"Coach Fitzgerald!" she yells. He eyes me, and I shrug.

Not sure why they're being picky about who they let in now.

A minute later, Demi runs over to us, looks at the color of my bib and frowns.

"I'm so sorry," she says, wrapping her arms around my neck. "My mom, she's just, God, I missed a race. I'm sorry."

"No problem." Although my gut feels like it's a problem. "Go, I don't want you to miss me at the bottom this time."

She presses her lips to mine, and yum, the taste of cherry makes me smile. Her tongue licks the seam of my lips and I never expected Demi to be so into PDA, but I go with it because she's a great fucking kisser. We're both heaving for breath when we separate.

"Trying to take all my reserve out of me. Are you

competing for one of these now?" I pretend to point around and a few of the guys laugh.

Demi laughs and that's what matters. I smack her ass, her missing the race long forgotten, a renewed energy inside of me. "Now, go."

Lucky for Demi, there's some controversy about times and lanes and bibs which gives her plenty of time to get down to the finish line. I fully anticipate kissing her again when I get down there.

Finally, everyone is ready and we're all grabbing the handles, our hips are rocking and it's time once again. My last race for this Winter Classics—my only chance at a medal.

I close my eyes. *Make it count.*

The gates go down and I fly out of the starting gate, down and up the first mound. I try to stay focused on the course, the turns, getting on the inside, passing my competition, but I keep tasting cherry, which reminds me of Demi. The way she purrs when my finger runs along her spine. Her soft breaths in and out after she comes. Her hand that lays on top of my stomach, fiddling with my treasure trail.

I'm much calmer when she's around. Usually, my brain is all go go go twenty-four seven, but when I'm with her, it hums like a smooth jazz song.

The same thing that happened during qualifiers happens to me at finals, except this time I see a body in front of me. I'm two turns from the end. Using all the physics and skills and experience I have, I get right on the edge of his board, coming up alongside him. We fly over the last hill, and his board travels over the line first, making me a silver medalist.

Damn Canadians. I don't live in an igloo so how do they expect me to compete?

I unclip my board, fist bumping and hugging the other racers and then I walk out the inflatable, Nik nodding at me. "I'll be with you in a second."

"If I stick around." I laugh.

Grady and Beckett are both watching me, wondering how I'll react. There are times I'd throw my board and swear at second place, but something is different this time around. Hell, maybe I'm maturing.

Jesus, that's a solemn thought.

Demi runs toward me, and I let my board fall to the side, so I can catch her when she jumps into my arms. "Congratulations!" She sprinkles kisses all over my face.

"What's this?" Grady asks with amusement.

"This is their agreement. The one where they sleep together and that's it," Beckett deadpans.

I raise my hand in the air, giving him the finger.

"Looks like the type of relationship where you kiss your boyfriend all over his face," Skylar adds, and I aim my finger in her direction.

Man, that felt good.

Demi falls from my arms but stays at my side. "Any other smart-ass comments?"

They all shake their heads, but I know what they're thinking. Hell, I'm thinking it, too, now.

Once that torch gets snuffed out, so does Demi and me.

CHAPTER SEVENTEEN

W e're at the restaurant and Soonil walks by, distributing another round of beers on the table. Well, six of them since Brandon has joined us. Demi's not drinking since she's the last to compete.

We all knock bottles and glasses. "Congratulations," they all say in unison.

"Thanks."

"Awe, is that a blush." Mia reaches forward, grabbing my cheek like I'm a child.

I smack it away as my phone starts ringing. I move in closer to Demi to check the screen. "I'll be right back."

She nods.

Heading outside I answer the phone. "Hey, Mom."

"Congratulations, baby."

My back hits the building and it slides down until I'm sitting on my heels.

"You watched."

A high-pitched laugh rings over the line. "Of course, silly, why would I not watch? Your brothers say congratulations, too."

"Are they there?"

"No, you know they have a lot going on, but they said they'd hit the highlights."

"Tell them thanks."

Thanks for nothing. They can't tell my nieces and nephews you're going to miss whatever to watch your uncle score a Winter Classics medal. What the fuck is that?

"When will you be home?" my mom asks.

Ah, the moment of truth. "I'm not sure yet. Within the next couple months or so. Do you need something?"

"No, we're good." She pauses which means there *is* something she needs. "So, since you got silver, does that mean less money from sponsors, or—"

Of course. Such bullshit. It all comes down to the money. How could I let myself get excited thinking that she was genuinely happy for me?

"No, I get the same."

"What happens if you decide not to compete in the next one?"

I frown. "Why are you so worried about my career?" I stand up, readying to chuck my phone in the garbage can. Then my mind shifts to Demi and me teaching her to throw baskets when she tosses something away and that brings a small smile to my lips.

"I just wanna make sure you're okay, that you have a future. You know how many athletes get hurt."

"Hey Mom, I gotta go. I'll call you later, okay?" I have my hand ready to pull the phone away from my ear, click the fucking red button and forget this call even happened.

"Wait... Dax."

I close my eyes, take in my last calming breath because it will be my last for a while.

"Yeah?"

"I hate to ask you this today of all days, but can you loan your mom some money? I'm behind on rent and your brothers say they're tapped out. You know I'm good for it."

I'll just add it to the tally that will get paid back never. "It'll be in your bank account tomorrow or the day after."

"Oh, baby, you're too good to your mama. I promise it will be the last time."

I roll my eyes. Sure it will.

"Anything else?" I ask.

"No, sweetie, talk to you later." She hangs up.

No 'I love you.' No 'congratulations again.' No 'I'm proud of you.' All she really gives a shit about is whether or not claiming silver is going to diminish my ability to help support her.

Tucking my cell phone into my pocket, I push my family issues aside. They'll be there until the day I go tits up. I should put a stop to it, but I'd probably give my mom my last dollar.

I head back into the restaurant thinking that my saving grace is the fact that I get to go taste Demi's lip balm. I'm smiling like a dude who's whipped as I weave through the crowd back to the table. My footsteps stop, spotting a dark-haired guy sitting in my vacant seat, chatting up my girlfriend.

Upon further inspection, I notice it's that French fuck, Julien or whatever his name is. Why the hell is he with her? How can she even entertain his company?

Breaking the distance, I stand at the edge of the table. "You're in my seat." I glare down at him.

He looks up, Demi's gaze follows. There's no guilty expression on her face. That's one good sign, I suppose. I'm not used to being on this end of things.

"Oh, hey, I heard congratulations are in order," Jackass says.

I stare blankly at him, waiting for him to get out of my seat.

"Julien was just leaving," Demi says, kicking the leg of the chair as a hint to Frenchie to get the fuck up.

"So, hop to it. Out of my seat." I grab the back of the seat, pulling it out a little.

"Dax," Demi says with concern in her voice.

"I asked politely the first time."

The rest of our friends are staring up at me. I'm positive the guys see the steam coming out of my ears. I want to body slam this guy. How does he think he can hit on Demi after everything he did?

Julien stands up, eye to eye with me, but muscle to muscle, I win.

Demi watches. "Thanks, Julien, I'll think about it."

"You'll think about what?" I look around Julien to Demi.

"Nothing," she says.

"It sounds like something."

"Hey, let's go outside." Beckett stands, placing his hand on my chest.

I grab his hand and drop it to his side. He looks over to Grady and Brandon for reinforcements. He doesn't want this to get out of hand, but I do. I'm jonesing for a fight after talking to my mom and Julien has a fucking stamp on his forehead that says, 'hit me.'

"You trying to get back in her pants?" I ask.

"Dax," Demi sighs.

Grady's chair screeches on the floor and the people around us are starting to notice the commotion and mill around.

"Because let's get something straight." I walk so I'm

chest to chest with him. "That position is filled...by my dick."

"Dax!" Demi slams her hand on the table.

"Holy shit," Skylar says, staring at Mia with huge eyes.

Mia smiles like she's got some kind of hidden secret she's been locking up for years and it's all finally coming out.

"Oh, really because I don't think she'd be thinking about my offer if you fulfilled all her needs," the idiot says.

"Get the fuck out." Grady places his hand in front of Julien.

He's too late because my fist is cocked back, ready to hit this motherfucker square in the jaw.

"No." Beckett grabs my arm.

Julien laughs, and I fight against my friend's restraint.

"She'll never go back to you," I say, and he continues to laugh squeezing Demi's shoulder before he leaves our area.

"I'm going to fuck him up," I yell at his retreating back.

Demi stands up, grabs my hand and yanks me, pulling me out of the restaurant in the other direction.

"Where are you taking me? My alpha side turn you on? Wanna quickie behind the building?"

She doesn't laugh. Actually, no one laughs except a guy we passed on the way out the door. He found my joke hilarious. As he should.

She pushes the door open and tosses me out. Well, I allow her to toss me because let's get something straight, if push came to shove, I've got about a hundred pounds on Demi.

"What the hell was that?" she points to the restaurant.

"Are you seriously going to go out with that vag badger again?"

She closes her eyes and shakes her head. "That what?"

"Vag badger." She just stares at me, so I continue. "You

know a guy who badgers a girl again and again until she lets him in her pants."

She inhales a deep breath and squeezes the bridge of her nose for second.

"After the way he treated you, you're actually considering seeing him again?"

Demi crosses her arms and I'll admit, I glanced at her pushed up tits. But only for a second.

"If I did go out with him, what concern is it to you?"

"What?"

She steps closer to me. "This is just sex, correct?" She waves a finger between us. "I can see other people, remember? Those were your words."

I wince at the memory but straighten my back. "You want to see him?" I grind out.

"That's not the point, Dax."

"It sounds like you want him. My cock not cutting it anymore?" A group of girls walking by giggle and run into the restaurant.

"Will you please quiet down." She steps closer to me again. "You made these rules."

"If I made them, I can change them."

She laughs. "You want to change the rules now? No doubt to benefit yourself."

I hook my finger into the waistband of her jeans and pull her toward me. She doesn't fight it and I didn't expect her to. Her face isn't holding that 'I hate you Dax' look I've seen enough times to recognize. "Can you not date anyone else until after the closing ceremonies?"

She rolls her eyes, her hands landing on my shoulders. "What are you going to give me if I agree?"

I nuzzle my head into her neck, licking up her throat. "Orgasms aren't enough?"

She shakes her head. "How about one dinner date?"

"Dinner?" I murmur into her soft skin.

"Dinner."

We've done dinner a zillion times together, so I'm surprised she didn't ask for more.

I pull back and shrug. "Sure."

She steps closer into my body.

"Tomorrow night, dinner."

"Can we go back to my room now?" I mumble in her ear. "I feel like make-up sex with you is going to be phenomenal."

She smacks my shoulder. "We barely fought. Maybe you should have make-up sex with Julien."

I lick my way up her throat to her mouth, hovering and staring at her bright green eyes. "You are so fucking hot when you're mad at me. I forgot what it was like when you hated me. Take me back to my room and punish me for being bad."

She laughs but doesn't decline. Instead, she links her hand with mine and we head in to grab our coats.

Ignoring the snide remarks, I go celebrate my silver medal with a few gold medal performances.

CHAPTER EIGHTEEN

With the silver medal under my belt, I head to the only place I want to be this morning—Demi's practice. The entire time I've known her, I've never seen her ski in person. I mean I have, but never paid much attention.

Hearing her mom's voice on my approach makes me happy I've stayed away until now. I have a feeling I'm going to have to bite my tongue and I've never been good at that.

"Demi, what are you doing? You have to take that last turn sharper." Her mom is shaking her head.

Demi hasn't seen me yet and inhales a big breath, unclips her skis and steps out of them.

"Carla, she's beating her time." One of the other coaches intervenes, no doubt this isn't the first occasion.

"She could do better. Her skis are cutting in and slowing her down."

Maybe I should be thankful my family never joins me at the Classics.

"She's tired. You can see it, same as I can. She needs a day of rest," the other coach argues.

I look at Demi to see her reaction to all this. I'm almost

positive she's not listening. Her hand is on her phone, her thumbs moving at hyper speed.

My phone dings in my pocket and all three heads swivel in my direction.

Demi smiles, taking off her helmet and tucking it under her arm as she walks over to me. "Hey," she says, without hesitation.

I tuck my hands into my jacket pockets and dip my head like I can hide out and only see her. "I thought I'd catch you at practice."

"It's not much fun." The snow crunches under her boots while she leaves her skis stranded by her coach.

My gaze flicks to her mom who's glaring at me.

"How much longer will you be? Maybe I can take you to lunch?"

A devilish smile crosses her lips and she glances over her shoulder. "About a half hour. I'd love to."

I nod.

"Demi?" Her mom's boots tread through the snow toward us.

"Hey, Mom, this is Dax. Dax Campbell. He's in snow-board cross. Won silver yesterday."

I look at her mom closely. She has a matching set of eyes with her daughter and if I wanted to know what Demi will look like in twenty years, I just have to study her mom's face —she has the same strawberry blonde hair, a few less freckles than Demi, but their eyes and their nose are both the same.

I hold my hand out and her mom shakes it, although daintily as if she's afraid I have something she'll catch. "Carla Harrison." Then she turns back to Demi. "We have to get going. You have two more practice runs."

Demi nods. "Dax is going to watch and then we're going to lunch."

Carla forces a smile. "How nice."

Demi glances back at me. "The sooner I'm done, the sooner we're out of here." She winks slyly so her mom doesn't notice.

They both walk away, and I don't think I've ever spoken less my entire life, but Carla Harrison is about as scary as Kathy Bates' character in Misery.

Demi's mom has a vice grip on her daughter's arm, pulling her away like she's a toddler who just ran off. I step forward, but Demi shoots me a smile over her shoulder before hopping on the snowmobile to take her back up the hill.

Figuring I have some time, I pull out my phone to read the text Demi sent me.

Demi: *Meet me in my room in an hour?*

A smile forms on my lips. She was thinking of me, just as I was thinking of her.

"So, Dax, are you the one tiring my daughter out?" Carla stands next to me at the bottom of the hill. I didn't even hear the woman approach. She's like a damn ninja. There are no accusations in her tone, so I'm hopeful that must mean something good.

I chuckle. "No, Ma'am."

She side eyes me.

I'm full of shit and she knows it.

"Now that your event is over, is your plan to monopolize the rest of my daughter's time?"

"No, Ma'am."

"Stop calling me Ma'am, I am not that old."

"Okay, then. No, Carla."

We're both still facing the hill. If anyone saw us from a distance they'd never think we were having a conversation.

"As you can see, Dax, I do *not* take this sport lightly. I'm a three-time medalist and if I have any say my daughter will be, too. Her entire life is skiing. I don't intend for that to change now."

"Believe me, Carla, I don't intend to alter Demi's dreams in any way."

She huffs. "Sure, you don't. But one thing will lead to the next and soon she'll be telling me that she's engaged and pregnant."

I chuckle to myself and she shoots me a look. One that if she had anything sharp on her, would cause me to fear for my life. I hold up my hands. "Your daughter and I are just friends."

"Friends? I may not be that old, Dax, but I'm old enough to know there's no such thing as a man and a woman just being friends."

"You don't have to believe me, but it's the truth."

I can't very well say, 'I'm screwing your daughter until the Classics are over and then you can have your workhorse back', now can I?

"I assume you're the one joining us for dinner tonight?" Carla asks.

My heart thumps in the chest. Dinner?

"The annual dinner we have before her race every Classics. It's a tradition and she asked that her father add one more to the reservation. I assume that's you?"

I swallow to coat my now dry throat. The dinner is with her parents? She might have mentioned that.

"Yes, I know about it and please thank Mr. Harrison for making room for me."

She rolls her eyes. "Mr. Harrison will be mighty surprised with you. However, he'll probably like you. I, on the other hand, see the distraction you and your *friendship* is on Demi. She might not realize it, but a man is the last thing she needs right now."

Demi carves out her stop at the bottom of the hill, pulling up her goggles immediately. I missed her skiing and I have Carla to blame for it.

"What'd you think?" she says, using her poles to pop out of her skis. She genuinely wants my opinion on her run.

"You look great." I'm not lying, the skin-tight lycra shows off all her curves, and the places I love to kiss.

"Thanks. Okay, one more."

"Demi," her mom says, jogging over to the snowmobile.

I can't hear the specific words, but I know she's judging her on the run which I don't really understand. She can only see the bottom half of it and she spent more time talking to me than watching her daughter. Not to mention, I want to tell Carla to bug off, but there's no way would I try to drive a wedge between Demi and her family. I know all too well what it's like to live without one.

CHAPTER NINETEEN

"Harder!" Demi screams, her thighs clenched so hard along my waist I fear loss of circulation in my toes.

I grind into her and her fingers grip the headboard behind her, keeping her body as stable as possible.

"Damn, how do you get better every time?" She stares up at me with lust-filled eyes and I can't hold myself back.

My hand slides to her neck, and I slam my lips to hers. Our kiss is ravenous and frantic, and we're unable to get our fill of one another.

She clenches around my cock, and I still inside of her, filling the condom. My lips slow, but don't leave hers, while my chest presses down on hers, my hands brushing the sweaty strands to the side. Never in my life have I come at the same time as my partner.

"So, when were you going to tell me about the dinner?" I ask after we've caught our breath.

A sly smile forms on her swollen lips. "My mom?"

I nod. "Your mom."

"Sorry." She bites her lip. I bend down, pulling it out from her teeth and licking the flesh. I love the taste of her.

"Were you afraid I wouldn't go?"

She looks to the side and I slowly pull out of her. "Maybe."

I chuckle. "You're probably right. I don't do parents."

She pushes on my chest and I roll over to my back. "You don't do parents? Who are you, James Dean?"

I chuckle, heading to the bathroom to dispose of the condom. "Parents don't really like me, and I can definitely confirm that your mom hates me."

When I return she's throwing my T-shirt over her bare chest and it doesn't escape me that it's the first time she's covered herself after sex. Lately, we've talked after or gone for a repeat.

I take a seat on the bed and when she crosses her legs, her knee brushes along my stomach. "My mom hates everyone. Don't take it personally."

I slide up so my back is against the headboard. I wonder if I just should've kept my mouth shut. "I have a feeling we come from very different backgrounds."

"People are people." Her finger runs down my thigh over the sheet. The fact she's trying to distract me from having this conversation says my assumptions are correct.

"Were you going to surprise them? Just walk in there with some blue-collar guy on your arm?"

Her jaw drops. Does she not see that she's the princess and I'm the help?

"Dax, my family isn't like that, and I was going to tell you this afternoon."

"In post-orgasmic bliss?"

"No, that's when you think clearly. I was going to ask you right before you came." She giggles, moving over to straddle me, and my hands mold to her hips.

"You didn't though."

She bends down and kisses my lips. "You were too good, and I forgot." She rests her forehead on mine.

"Now I know you're using all your sexual skills to persuade me."

"You have such a big and powerful cock, I couldn't even remember what I wanted to tell you."

I roll her over and trap her hands above her head while she laughs. "Ask me nicely," I order her.

"Dax Campbell, will you go to dinner with my family tonight?"

My eyes swim with hers, amusement and lust swirled together in her green hues. How could I say no to her beautiful face? "I'd love to."

"Love to?" She raises one eyebrow.

"Well..."

I lower my mouth to hers and I push away the gut-churning fact I'll be meeting her dad tonight.

Fuck buddies aren't supposed to play meet the parents, are they?

———

WEARING the one suit I brought for the sponsor's gala before the games, I knock on Demi's door.

The door swings open right away, and Skylar is standing there with her hair in a high bun, sweatpants and a T-shirt on.

"Prince Charming," she says. Nothing in her voice sounds cheery or remotely like a Disney movie.

"Wicked Stepmother." I nod and walk in without waiting for her invitation.

"I'll be right there," Demi says, peeking out of the bathroom.

She pauses, a slow smile forming on her lips. "You look great."

We share a moment of locked gazes and since all I've seen is her head, I anticipate seeing the rest of her.

"What are you doing tonight?" I ask Skylar. "Quality time with Hoff? Maybe a chick flick, do each other's makeup, pillow fight?"

She scowls at me. If she stopped giving me the judgmental looks all the time I'd be nicer.

"We're watching movies and ordering food."

I nod, not even worth my energy.

"You can cut the jokes, you know." She sits on the edge of her bed close to me and lowers her voice. "I know you seem to think that guys and girls can't be friends, but they can and it's a hell of a lot safer than what you and Demi are doing."

"Demi and I are in agreement with what we're doing."

She rolls her eyes. "That's why you won't let her go out with Julien? The reason you puffed out your chest like a lion protecting your lioness?"

Demi's busy singing to some song playing over her phone in the bathroom. "What do you care?"

I could tell Skylar that she's right. I was jealous as hell when Julien was sniffing around and it brought out something I would have been better caging, but we're past that point now. I don't know any better than Demi what's happening between us, but we have an agreement and I intend to enjoy it.

"I care because she's my friend and I don't want to see what happened after the last Classics, happen this time."

"We had a miscommunication last time. This time we're on the same wavelength."

Again with the eye roll. What are they, marbles?

"Well." She pats my leg. "Let me fill you in on some things since you like to speak your unrequested advice. Fuck buddies don't spend the night together, they don't go to dinners, they don't ice bruises, and they sure as hell don't meet the parents."

She stands up, grabs her jacket, and puts her feet in her boots, poking her head into the bathroom, she exchanges words with Demi about having fun and how she'll see her tomorrow.

I stand there dumbfounded and then glance to the door where Skylar shoots me a tight-lipped smile that implies I should think about what I'm doing. Can I really blame her? I don't want Demi to be upset either.

"Ready."

I turn toward the bathroom door and my mouth drops. I want to say I've never seen someone so beautiful. She's dressed in a blue dress that's fitted to the waist, flaring out over her long thin legs. It's more conservative than other dates I've had, but she's sexy as all hell in it.

Who knew that leaving more to the imagination could be hot as fuck?

I wonder what she's wearing under it?

"That bad?" she asks, her lips turned up into a grin.

I shake my head, standing and linking my hand with hers before pulling her into me. "Not bad one bit. Gorgeous. Breathtakingly gorgeous."

The blush I've become so familiar with creeps up her neck and floods her cheeks. "Thank you."

"You're welcome." I will my gaze to leave hers, but until she reaches past me for her coat, I don't even realize I've been creepy the way I've been taking her in.

"Here." I take the coat, holding it out for her.

She slides her arms through the sleeves and I place a kiss on the back of her neck before covering it with the coat.

I hold out my arm like the gentleman I am not, and she happily threads her arm through mine.

"Let's go meet the parents."

She smiles, but there's a tentativeness there I never noticed before, which only makes that gnawing in my stomach worse.

CHAPTER TWENTY

D inner is at the restaurant in her parents' hotel. It's supposed to serve American food and it's a tad more elegant than the way I usually dine, but it's not outside of my comfort zone.

We check our coats and head to the hostess stand. Demi gives the hostess her last name, but I spot her mom waving us over. I'm not sure what I expected, but I didn't expect this. There are more than just her parents here.

Demi grips my hand harder as we approach. The entire table stands and begins clapping. Demi elegantly moves around the table, hugging and kissing the cheeks of who I assume are grandparents, aunts, uncles, and cousins. All these people took time out of their lives to come support her.

When she's finished making the rounds, she stands to the side of her chair and glances over at me. "This is Dax Campbell, he just won silver at snowboard cross."

The fact she announces me as a medalist already has me wondering if she thinks that would make a difference as to how I was treated tonight. I try to push back my fears and insecurities of being at a table with people who never in their life have had money problems.

"Dax, this is my dad, Ashton Harrison, Junior."

Her dad smiles, stands and holds out his hand. "Pleasure to meet you, Dax."

He seems friendly enough, I dissect his features trying to find one that matches Demi, but our introduction is over too soon.

I shift my hand to Carla. "Nice to see you again, Carla."

She smiles, and again with the dainty handshake. "Nice to see you," she says with a look like she's chomping down on shards of glass.

We all sit down, Demi pointing out all her family members while I exchange waves with them.

"And this is my grandma, Pearl," she points to the elderly woman next to me.

She smiles a sweet grandmotherly grin with a light but welcoming handshake. "I'm Ashton's mom."

"Nice to meet you."

"Nice to meet you," her tone slightly more seductive than the way I said it. I had to hear that wrong, right?

The waitress comes over and takes our drink orders. Demi just finished ordering a seltzer water with a lime when her mother speaks up.

"Oh, Demi, you know how carbonation makes you. Maybe just distilled water."

Demi turns back to the waitress. "Distilled water with lime."

"Oh, maybe lemon," Carla says. "I know sometimes limes give you heartburn."

"It's fine, Mom." Demi looks to the waitress. "Lime, please."

The waitress nods and looks over to me, but I'm not

about to drink when she has to endure this meal sober. "Same."

"No." Demi shakes her head, looking to the waitress. "He'll have a Miller Lite."

"No, I won't. Distilled water with lime sounds great." I lick my lips and Demi laughs, her head falling to my shoulder.

"You didn't have to," she says under her breath.

"I want to."

She gives me one of those you're-my-hero looks that I'm really starting to love. They almost make me believe that maybe I could be a hero to her.

"So, Dax, silver? That's quite an accomplishment," her dad says from across the table.

I nod and shift in my seat when I find Carla's eyes scrutinizing Demi and me.

"Yeah, I mean I wanted gold of course, but I can't really complain about silver."

"Gold is the best," Carla says.

If you hadn't already guessed those three medals Carla won? All gold.

"Well, Carla, as you know from being an athlete in the Classics as well, sometimes you work hard and just don't get gold," I say.

Her eyes narrow. "You were gold last time, correct?"

So, I wasn't the only one googling.

"I did."

"Do you think you got silver because you were more distracted this time?"

"Mom, let it go," Demi interrupts.

My hand slides under the table and I squeeze her leg, reassuring her that I can take care of this.

"I think we only get one life. And for me, I've always

wanted to live it. Was I disappointed I didn't get gold? Of course. I wouldn't be here if I was okay being second best, but I also wouldn't change anything that's happened this Classics." I squeeze Demi's leg again to reassure her that she wasn't a distraction to me. Furthest thing from the truth.

"Well, you and Demi only have a few more of your top years left to compete."

Is that seriously her comeback?

"True, all the more reason I'm not going to beat myself up about silver. I'm going to work harder this off-season and come back stronger and faster for the next Classics."

"That's good thinking, Dax," Ashton says. "I tell Carla all the time to just relax and enjoy it. Her daughter followed in her footsteps, what more could you ask for?" He smiles, raising his drink in the air.

"Ashton was never a competitor, so he doesn't understand," Carla fires back. "Spreadsheets and numbers don't bring the same sense of achievement as a gold medal does." She slides her hand to the back of his head, massaging his neck.

"What is it you do, Mr. Harrison?" I ask.

"Ashton, please. I'm an investment banker."

I nod, not really understanding the ins and outs of what an investment banker does and not really wanting to.

"I assume my work would seem boring to someone who races down mountains." He almost seems ashamed of his profession, but from what I can tell from the size of the ring on Carla's finger and the overall outward appearance of them, he does well and should be proud of himself.

"Well, we all have different things that make us tick, right?" I say.

He smiles, raising his glass once more. "I like you, Dax."

Demi's hand links with mine and she squeezes.

"Me, too." Grandma Pearl surprises me by placing her head on my shoulder. "You seem good for Demi. Calm her down a bit."

"Thanks, Grandma." Demi looks past me to her grandma.

"Sweetie, you're just strung too tight like your mother. You need to loosen up and it seems like this lug could unravel you." Her voice sounds almost seductive. I crack my neck, thinking I must be hearing things.

"Oh, Pearl, Demi is fine," Carla says.

Pearl rolls her eyes, and Carla moves on to talk to the waitress about dinner.

"Someone needs to pull the stick from her ass," Pearl whispers in my ear and my eyes widen, but I try to keep my cool.

I choke out a laugh and Pearl laughs outright, not caring who hears her.

Things with the family are going well, our drinks come, and a meal Carla planned for everyone—some specialty item that would be good for Demi. The only thing halfway appealing is the pasta side dish.

Demi excuses herself, going down the table to talk to her cousins. They're younger, and she sits and colors with them for a bit. They ask her questions about how fast she goes down the hill and she even points to me to say I race people down the hill, too. They all look over with slack jaw expressions like I'm their favorite Disney star.

"So, Dax, may I ask how you invest all your money?" Ashton's question throws me off a little. "I'm sure you have a guy, but I feel like it's my duty to make sure athletes don't spend all their money and end up with nothing. You guys work hard for it, but you wouldn't believe how many professional athletes end up bankrupt." He leans back in his chair, and one of Demi's uncles comes over and joins the conversation.

"I've heard that about professional athletes. Hard to believe," her uncle says.

Carla, thank God, is talking to the waitress again. Hopefully she tips well.

"I'm good." My stomach tightens. Not like I'd tell him I give loans to my family with no interest and no plans of ever being repaid.

"So, you got a guy?" he winks. "Good boy."

He turns to the other guy. "I've set Demi up nicely. Of course, she doesn't even know how to get to her money." He laughs and the feeling in the pit of my stomach has me excusing myself to the bathroom.

I stand in the bathroom, knowing if someone were at this table they'd know one thing isn't like the other. He set her up nicely. Probably made her winnings triple, whereas my mom is calling to see if by getting silver she'll get less from me every month.

I'm not desolate, hell, I've done better than any member of my family, but Demi is on another level. Like the cheerleader in high school—she's an untouchable, beautiful girl who no one deserves, especially the burnout who cuts class to head to the slopes.

We're done eating, so this night should be over soon.

Just get through it a little longer.

After tomorrow Demi's event will be over and there's no reason for us to hook-up anymore. I could leave and go home.

I can't stand to think of how the thought of that makes me feel, so I do what I do best. Push the feeling to the side and open the door to head back to the table.

"Hey, you." Demi steps out from under the light in the dark hallway. Like an angel. Not my angel though.

She walks right into me, arms sliding to my back. I hug her to me, her warmth always something I enjoy too much. With her chin resting on my chest and staring up at me she says, "Thank you. I know tonight isn't easy."

I shrug.

"I selfishly asked you because I didn't want to deal with questions from my aunts and grandma about guys and how I'm getting older."

I chuckle, my hand running up and down her back. "It's fine. Your mom is a tad intense, but..."

Her arms tighten. "More than a tad."

"Can I take you home soon?"

She lets her hands slide down, grabbing my ass. "Yes." She rises up on her tiptoes kissing my neck. A move that's become like crack to me. I can't get enough. "I have some nervous energy I need to dispense before my race tomorrow."

"I don't think your mother would approve." She links her hand in mine, pulling me down the hall.

"My mother doesn't know what you're hiding under those pants."

We're both laughing as we walk up to the table to say our goodbyes.

We leave the restaurant and all those feelings of how I'm not worthy of her disperse when I'm buried deep inside of her and she's calling out my name.

CHAPTER TWENTY-ONE

The weather is warmer today, which means the bottom of the hill could cause some problems for the skiers. I stand at the bottom because I can't be up on top with her— her mother might push me down the hill.

"Hey, has she been up yet?" Mia comes up alongside me, giving me a kiss on the cheek.

"No," I say nodding with my head at the hill. "There's still three skiers before her."

"Hey, man." Grady fist bumps me.

Another skier shows up on the giant screen. Not Demi, but the three of us watch her come down the course. She's fast, although I don't know everything it takes to make a great downhill skier, her time overtook the first place.

"Two more and she's up," Mia says, and leans back against Grady's chest. His arms come around her so that she's firmly wrapped in his grip. Those two couldn't be more lovesick.

"We haven't missed her, right?" Skylar runs up to our group huffing and puffing, stopping next to me.

"I forgot how hard this one is to get to." Beckett, who

seems equally as exasperated as Skylar, stands alongside her.

"No. There's two more to go before her." Mia gives the wicked witch the information she seeks.

"Hey," Skylar elbows me and I look down at her. "I'm sorry." With a fleeting look at Beckett, she focuses back on me. "I know we're on the same side, so..." she places her hands in the air, "backing off."

I nod. She had some fair points. Points I haven't forgotten.

I've known for a while that Demi and me have been crossing a line—that we're more like a loving couple than fuck buddies. The notion of her being my lucky charm hasn't been my motivation for wanting to hang out with her for a while now. But I'm still the guy who doesn't want a permanent address. I don't want to settle down and have two point five kids in the suburbs and spend my day at a desk job. Demi deserves what her mom found. To be able to go into any store and buy whatever she wants. To go on luxury vacations filled with expensive dinners with extravagant jewelry around her neck. Someone predictable and responsible and give her all the things that she needs.

"Thank you," I say. "Is it gonna be hard to bite back your words?"

She elbows me in the ribs. Fucking hard.

"We'll just forget it happened."

She focuses in front of her. Beckett looks at me over her head with his I'm-the-legend grin on his face for getting Skylar to apologize. Maybe he is because Skylar reminds me of myself a little and I rarely apologize for anything.

While all this is going on I miss another racer, but she doesn't make the winner's board.

The five us stand there in silence. One more racer before Demi and my heart starts thumping in my chest.

"Where's Salty?" I ask anyone who will answer because I need to redirect my attention to anything other than the fact that Demi's next.

"He's busy." Grady waggles his eyebrows suggestively.

Mia elbows him in the gut.

"You can't get mad, he watches us together and says nothing."

Mia turns to me, a look of annoyance on her face. "The girl is like...so not good enough for him."

Grady laughs, and Mia elbows him again. "You're hitting a little too low there. You do want kids one day, right?"

Like someone turned on a light switch, Mia turns around, her arms stretched to the back of his head, her eyes looking up at him lovingly. "You want some?"

Grady glances at me for a second with the biggest grin on his face. Then he fixates back on Mia. "Of course. I want to see what me and you together looks like."

She jumps into his arms and plants her lips to his. Grady's everything I'm not. Mia would nail him here on the hill for saying he wants kids. Another checkmark in the wrong column for Demi and Dax being right for each other.

"Here she is." Skylar hits my arm.

What is it with these women?

Demi's at the top, she circles her neck around, positions her poles and her eyes shut briefly, her head moving like she's mentally going through the course.

"You got this, girl," I whisper to myself as I stare up at the screen.

The announcer crackles and fades, but I catch Harrison. She leaves the gate, her body bending, her skis flaw-lessly moving down the line.

"Great one," Grady says.

She's under the mark at the halfway point, already beating the first-place pace.

"I have no idea how she does this. I'd close my eyes the entire way down," Mia says, her arm now entwined in mine, her hand on my forearm.

"She loves speed," Skylar says.

All their voices fade into background noise.

"That's it. Don't overdo it," I say quietly.

My gut clenches as she takes a turn that looks like she could lose her footing at any moment.

"You're the best, baby. The gold is yours."

She's coming into view on the mountain, so I shift my eyes from the television screen to her and I watch with a dry mouth and lump in my throat as she comes through the hardest area.

She lands her jump with minimal air. It's hard to process anything completely because of how damn fast she's moving.

"That's it. She had to have done it." My heart finally beats again as she crosses the line.

Demi carves to a stop, moving her goggles off her eyes and staring at the screen. A minute later, the time comes up and she's number one. With fifteen other skiers behind her, she knows there's a chance she could get overtaken, but my gut says she's got it.

She glances around the crowd and her eyes find me.

"Congratulations," I mouth.

Her smile grows wider and she unclips from her skis and heads through the inflatable.

"Look who's talking to themselves now?" Mia says, a cocky grin on her face.

Ignoring her, I weave my way through all the people, grabbing my girl by the waist and swinging her around.

Carla looks on with a scowl, but whatever because her dad and grandma have smiles on their faces.

"You did it!"

She laughs. "Not yet. We'll see."

I lower her to the ground, the spandex of her jumpsuit sliding easily down my body. "You'll be on the center podium." I wink.

Our friends come and swallow her up with congratulations. I watch from afar, her eyes seeking me out every now and then. For the first time ever, I wish I could be one of those guys who could work twelve hours a day in an office and had an appreciation for white picket fences.

CHAPTER TWENTY-TWO

Demi ended up claiming gold last night and we all went out to celebrate, including her mom who somehow managed not to strangle me. Even after a few drinks.

I'm not sure when this friends-with-benefits thing is supposed to have run its course, but I do know I'm not ready for it to end. Which is why I've dragged my ass out of bed this morning, so Demi and I can figure it out.

I approach Demi's door, a pathetic pussy-whipped smile already creasing my lips.

"No, that's not Dax." I hear Demi's voice talking to someone and I wonder who it is because I thought Skylar said she was going to back the fuck off from us. Let us work this out ourselves. It's foreign terrain for me. The least she could've done is give me a fucking minute to talk to Demi about everything.

"He has no money. He doesn't do this for the love of his country. How could you actually like him?" The French accent tells me that fucking vag badger is back, front and center trying to get back into Demi's pants. Pants he zipped firmly up himself before the Classics when he decided quantity was better than quality.

"You don't even know him."

That's my girl.

"I don't need to know him. His reputation speaks for itself. He almost hit me in that restaurant. He's a complete Neanderthal. Come on, mon amour. We were good together."

My fists clench at my sides and I step forward, my hand inches from pushing the door farther open.

"You have no idea. Did you know that he sends most of his earnings home to help out his family, even though they want nothing to do with him unless it involves a blank check?"

The creaking of the bed is the sound I hear when my heart breaks for the first time ever.

She told him. The secret that no one knows. How could she betray me?

"Now get the fuck away from me," she says in a disgusted voice.

I push the door open. Demi's eyes widen, and Frenchie bolts up from his seated position.

"Am I interrupting?" I rein my temper in enough to get rid of this jackass before I pummel him into the ground.

Why do I even care that she told him? This is exactly what we needed—something to keep us away from one another since we were bound to implode anyway.

"You didn't interrupt anything. Julien was just leaving." Demi shoots him a look and he snickers.

"I underestimated you, Campbell." He steps forward, slowly leaving the room. "Next Classics I guess I'll get myself my own lucky charm. Screw her to improve my performance and win first place."

He snickers and without thinking, I grab his shirt before he can flee the room and slam his back into the wall.

"Watch it," I grind out. Adrenaline is pumping through my veins at a hundred times the rate it does when I'm at the starting gates.

"What is he talking about?" she says to me. "What are you talking about?" she asks Julien when I don't answer.

I grip his shirt tighter, sliding him higher up the wall.

"Dax went after you because he thought you were his lucky charm. He won gold last Classics when he was fucking you and thought it might work this time around, too. I guess not since he only won silver."

I cock my fist back and nail him in the cheekbone.

"Dax!" Demi steps forward, planting her hand on my forearm. "Go, Julien." She points to the door.

"At least I fucking medaled, you piece of shit tenth place," I yell out the door behind him.

"Tell me he's lying."

I turn back around, Demi's arms are crossed, her eyes lasered in on me.

"First, we're gonna talk about you telling him all about my family shit. Out of all the people in the world, why would I ever want him to know?"

Her arms drop, her eyes morphing into that sympathetic, pitiful look I hate. I don't need anyone feeling sorry for me. I have a fucking fantastic life.

"I just..."

"You wanted to explain how you could like a Neanderthal like me?"

"No." She steps forward with her hand out, but I step back, pushing my hands through my hair. "You have it wrong. I just—"

"Save it, Demi."

I'm so angry right now and I'm not even sure I know what I'm so pissed about. Her spilling my secret? At Julien? Whatever it was between her and I ending? At myself for falling for her? All of it? None of it?

"You're not even going to listen to me?" Tears well in her eyes and I can't deny that my stomach knots and the impulse to want to make it better for her is strong.

"This was fun while it lasted anyway, right? Who cares now?" I shrug.

Her body slumps and her eyes shift into the saddest puppy dog expression. "You're ending this? Now?"

"Why do you sound surprised? You knew what this was. Our events are over."

"I guess I thought..."

"That'd I change my mind? That I'd suddenly change my ways and say I love you or some shit like that? Well, this time that's on you. My intentions were clear from the get-go. This isn't a damn fairy tale."

"You were clear?" That puppy dog in her eyes turns K-9. "I don't recall you asking me to be your lucky charm." Her fists are clenched at her sides and I think she'd like nothing more than to haul off and pop me one in the eye.

"That's not it," I say.

"It's not? Then why the hell does Julien think that and why didn't you tell him it's bullshit then? What am I, some joke in the locker room? Look how Dax got Demi to buy into his antics." A tear slips down her cheek and my own defenses slip. "He sure duped her this time." She wipes the tear off her cheek angrily.

"That's not how it went."

I step forward, losing any fight after seeing her like this.

Her arm flies forward, her finger pointing to the door. "Get out, Dax! You're right. Our events are over. We can move on with our lives. I'm sorry I couldn't get you to gold again this year, but hey, there's always the next Classics."

"Don't do this, Demi. Let me explain."

She stops and lets her arm fall to her side, and for a moment I think maybe we'll talk this out, but she lowers her head, looking at the ground. "Dax." She picks up her head, squaring her shoulders and looking me straight in the eyes. "Do you ever want to be in a relationship?"

Here it is, the expiration stamp landing on our papers. "No. But it's not you, it's me."

"Leave," she says with a strangled whisper.

I'd rather have her angry. Tear at my clothes, hit me, do anything but use that soft heartbroken voice that breaks me in two.

Five minutes ago, I was on my own mission to end this and now I want nothing more to stay and make it better. I feel fucking schizophrenic.

But I'll just make it worse if I stay. Our parting was inevitable.

So, I back out of the room, shutting the door behind me. Something crashes on the back of the door and with my head down and hands in my pockets, I head to my room.

How the fuck did I end up the heartbroken one?

CHAPTER TWENTY-THREE

I stuff my shit into my suitcase, not bothering to fold any of my clothes. My phone drops to the floor from the edge of the bed. It's been vibrating more than a dildo since the fight between Demi and me. The news must've dropped since Beckett's been blowing up my phone like he's dying.

Snatching my phone from the carpet, I freeze at the sight of her earring sitting there. A silver stud with diamonds wrapped around a red stone. My ass falls to the ground, wedged between Grady's bed and mine, and I pick up the only small piece of her I have left and stare at it like a lovesick fool.

It's a symbol that shows how out of my league she is, but I had her, under my hands and I know she enjoyed it. Not just the sex but our time together—the laughing and close-ness we shared. We both enjoyed it, but she was supposed to be insignificant to me.

I stand up, figuring I can have Beckett give it to Skylar once I'm long gone. Or I'll shove it under her door. What-ever, I'll go home and act the part of country boy hero and then jet to Europe or maybe a beach to blow off some steam.

The door opens and slams on the spring on the inside wall. If it weren't for that doorstop, the doorknob would now be firmly embedded in sheetrock.

"Goddammit, what the hell is your problem?" Beckett storms in, his voice so loud a few people passing by stare in to see what the deal is.

"Nothing. What's wrong with you?"

A little deflection never hurt anyone.

"I thought for sure she was it for you. That the whole lucky charm shit would shift and you'd figure out that someone can care for you and it's okay for you to care for someone else."

He sits down on Grady's bed. I'm surprised Skylar's not in tow ready to rip my balls off and feed them to me.

"I don't do relationships, Hoff. You know me. I'm not meant to be locked down."

He rolls his eyes, and I disappear into the bathroom to grab my shit from there.

"This whole macho I don't do relationships, is getting pretty old. You know that, right?"

"You can't possibly be giving me advice on this subject?" I throw my deodorant and hair gel into the bag.

"It's different for Skylar and me. We're good as friends. She's my family."

"I know what I'm doing," I say.

"Fucking hell, listen to me before you make the biggest mistake of your life."

Never in all the years I've known Beckett has his face been so red. I've never seen him so determined to change my mind about something. He's always the one who shrugs, says I see it differently and we move forward.

"What do you want me to do? Run down the hallways, sliding around corners in slow motion while music plays in the background? Knock on her door and fall to my knees? Tell her how much I love her and can't live without her? Sorry, brah, not me."

He stands up. "You know what? I'm out." Beckett rounds Grady's bed, but stops and turns around before he leaves. "When I first met you, I was instantly drawn to you. You're a fun guy who yeah, says stupid shit sometimes, but you've been there for all your friends. You're a best friend to everyone and are the glue that keeps us together. I know how families and growing up can screw with you. Trust me, I know. But Dax, you're worthy of love. Demi sees something in you. You see something in her. Don't be stupid and destroy it out of fear that you're not enough for her or that you might get hurt or whatever the fuck else it is you're scared of."

He walks out of the room slowly, probably hoping that I'll stop him, confess to him that he's right.

"She deserves it all, Beckett, and I'm not that guy."

"How do you know what she wants in life? Have you bothered to ask her?" He pauses for a second, so I can let his question sink in. "A girl who flies down an icy hill at eighty miles per hour doesn't scream housewife and PTA president to me."

The door shuts behind him as he leaves and as much as I try to ignore them, his words resonate. He's right about two things. She's not the type. Nothing about her says she wants a cookie cutter life. She took me to her parents knowing I wasn't like them. She was never standoffish or any different with me after I confessed how messed up my family is.

And he's right about me being scared. I've spent all my life avoiding heavy emotions, but I can't run from how I feel about Demi. And when I'm scared and backed into a corner —I attack.

Fuck, I am a dick.

A knock sounds on my door and I jump up to open it, hoping it's her so we can both apologize for the stupid shit we said.

I open the door and immediately back up when Skylar's finger hits my chest.

"I knew not to listen to Beckett. He sees the good in everyone. I knew you'd hurt her and now I have to pick up the pieces. Again." Her voice raises the farther she gets in my room. Her little dagger of a finger in constant motion against my chest.

I raise my hands. "I know. I know."

"You know nothing. You know how lucky you had it? What an amazing find she is?"

"I know, Skylar."

"If you knew, you'd be down there groveling for her forgiveness, which she wouldn't give because you're a jack-ass. Do you hear me? Total jackass!"

"I heard you, but Sky, I know. I'm going to make it right."

She stops poking me and narrows her eyes. "How so?"

"I haven't had a second to figure it out."

Her scrutiny doesn't falter. "Hmm...you like her?"

I nod.

"You want to be *with* her and not just in her pants?"

I nod.

"If she says no sex, you're still cool with being with her?"

I nod.

"You won't pull this bullshit again?"

I shrug.

"Yeah, true. You're Dax Campbell." She nails me in the chest with her pointer finger again. "Hurt her again and when you open that door, I'm going to punch you in the balls so hard, they'll be blue for weeks."

I roll my eyes. I'm not sure Skylar has that in her, but I'll let her believe it because the last thing I ever plan on doing is hurting Demi again.

"Deal."

She backs off, looking me over, still examining me to see if I'm telling the truth or not. I kind of deserve it, so I'll let her.

"What's your plan?" She eyes the suitcase. "You're leaving?"

"Not anymore and if I had a minute to think, I could come up with a plan."

"It has to be really big because she's really hurt, Dax." Skylar isn't saying it to be mean, she's being truthful and that's when I know exactly how to win her back.

"I've got a great idea."

I pray this is the one time that statement doesn't come back to haunt me and actually ends up being true.

CHAPTER TWENTY-FOUR

The karaoke bar is packed. Now that most of the events are over, the athletes that stuck around are looking for some action. And tonight, isn't duet night.

Demi sits at a table up front, Skylar on one side of her, a full table on the other. Which is perfect because that'll make it hard for her escape when I get up on stage.

She's got a drink in her hand, but no smile on her face. Actually, she looks like she'd rather be knitting than sitting here. Mia or Grady say something, and she turns, so I hurry to hide behind a guy. Not that I think she can see me with the crowd being so thick tonight, but I don't want to take any chances. I throw back a shot and hand the bartender some won.

Right now, the girl up on stage singing "Hello" by Adele should be thankful she's an athlete because she has no singing career ahead of her. Not that I should throw stones with what I'm about to do.

I'm supposed to be next, but Demi stands up, sliding by Skylar. Skylar grabs her arm, pulling her back down to her seat. She shakes her head, looking through the crowd. Of course, she'd figure out why she's here. My girl is a smart cookie.

Weaving through the crowd, I jump on stage interrupting the Adele wannabe. She stops mid-song, letting the mic fall from her mouth.

"Yeah, sorry, but this is a life or death situation," I say in her ear.

She still stares at me confused, her eyebrows drawn and a frown on her face.

"I promise you get next song and can have a redo."

The crowd boos. Man, they're ruthless. I pray they're kinder to me.

She leaves the stage, handing me the microphone. I look to the guy running the show and he nods.

She stands, her eyes glued to me.

"Stay," I say to Demi.

Mia spits out her beer all over the table when she spots my get-up. Grady's chair slides back and Beckett grabs a stack of napkins to clean up.

"Go Bieber. He looks like you, Hoff."

I throw my hair back, the long strands on my forehead already annoying the shit out of me. How does Bieber deal with this hairstyle? The sooner I can get her back, the sooner I can use some gel.

Skylar stands at Demi's side, whispering something to her. Our eyes are locked and the music starts.

"You're shittin' me, right?" Mia slaps the table, and I can tell that she's been celebrating a little too much tonight.

Grady shakes his head, leaning back in his chair with his arms across his chest. I'm surprised he doesn't have his camera out yet.

Still no smile from Demi.

"Sorry" by Justin Bieber starts playing and I sing the first verse straight to her.

She's still stiff as a board, nothing about her body language telling me that she's open to my apology.

Hello? I'm making a fool of myself here.

When the second verse begins, I up the stakes, my hand reaching down for hers.

She shakes her head.

Skylar gently nudges her, and she stumbles a step forward. Not letting my hand leave as I continue to sing the song to her, she finally relents, and I guide her up onto the stage, seating her on the chair.

During the song, I do the few dance moves I tried to master this afternoon. She lets me get close, only the microphone separating us without pulling away. My hand cradles her cheek and then I step back and do a few more moves.

God, I hope no one is recording this.

The song eventually ends, and I fall to my knees, looking up at her with the microphone still on.

"Demi Harrison, I'm an idiot. You're the best thing to ever enter my life and it scared me. When I'm scared, I do stupid shit, like thinking you were just a lucky charm to me. You are my lucky charm, but only because you believe in me." My head goes back and forth. "Not that the sex isn't off the charts." I wink.

She smiles.

"But it was more than that between us. And I want us to be more. Can you forgive me?"

She sits there silent, staring down at me. No tears, no emotion. Shit, she's not going to accept my apology. The silence goes on and the crowd starts mumbling.

Demi falls to her knees in front of me and holds my

head in her hands. "I wondered when you'd come to your senses."

"That's a yes?"

She nods. "I was pissed off Dax, but after I calmed down and talked to Beckett and Skylar, I realized you were just scared and needed time to sort yourself out. Still, I had to scare you a little, but when you hopped on this stage dressed like Justin Bieber, you were forgiven."

I let the microphone drop and it makes a horrible screeching noise, but I don't care, planting my lips on her until her back is on the stage.

"Usual place?" she asks, lust in her eyes.

"Never again. I'm taking you to my bed."

I sit up, ignoring the whistles and hold my hand out for her. She rises to her feet.

"Never?" There's disappointment in her voice.

"Well, not never, but definitely not tonight. I need you in a bed because I fully intend on exhausting you."

She giggles in the way that's like an electrical current right between my legs. "Come on."

"Leaving so soon?" Mia sing-songs as I weave us through the crowd.

When we get outside, I lead her to the side of the building. "I want to show you something, but take it as a good thing, okay?"

She stands there, and I lift my shirt, tearing the white bandage away from the skin on my chest to reveal a four-leaf clover.

"This Classics *you* were the best thing. Not the sex, or the fact that I won silver. Just you. You are my lucky charm, Demi, but in life. Not on the hill."

A single tear slips from her eye. "I love it. Thank you."

I cup her cheek, urging her forward. "I'm so sorry," I

whisper, my forehead resting on hers.

"Are you turning sentimental on me? I thought you were going to exhaust me?" She reaches and grabs my hand, pulling me away from the building.

"Can I ask you what your views are on being a Girl Scout leader?"

She laughs, turning around and grabbing my other hand. "Well, I always saw myself more as the PTA president."

I stop in my tracks and she glances over her shoulder, coyly smiling.

"I gotta keep you on your toes, Campbell." She winks.

I pick her up, swinging her around in the air. "I'll never be scared again."

Her lips dip down. "Then I have something to tell you...I'm pregnant."

"What?" My voice drops to a whisper. I wore a condom every damn time.

"Jeez, I thought you were going to banter back and forth with me. I sure hope you haven't changed, Dax because I really liked you the way you were. Minus how insane you act when you're scared shitless about your feelings." She gives me a chaste kiss on the lips. "Don't go turning into a stiff on me."

"Well, I'm stiff." I push my hips forward. "Is that what you mean?"

"There you go." She smiles.

I stop in the middle of the village when a light snowfall begins falling from the sky.

"Never stop challenging me," I say.

She smiles up at me like I'm a rock star and with her in my arms, I feel like I am. "Promise."

My lips fall to hers to seal our *new* deal.

EPILOGUE
DEMI

"Thanks, Eva." I hear Dax talking to the waitress as I approach from the outside.

She leaves with an empty bottle of beer and my glass. I smile. "Thank you."

"I'll be right back," she says.

I enter the cabana. Dax looking like he should be posing for a magazine cover. He's tanned from our time in Thailand, his six-pack is on display, and his happy trail is leading to the prize below his board shorts.

When he sees me, he shoots me a smile that literally weakens my knees. Sometimes I can't believe he's mine. I can kiss him, seduce him, smack him playfully whenever the urge strikes—which is often.

"Already shortening the waitress' name?" I ask, sitting down on his lap.

"She asked me to?" He honestly worries that I thought he'd flirt with her.

She's cute and all, but I don't bother worrying about Dax straying. He had his choice and out of all the women he's ever had, he chose me.

I giggle, falling into his chest. His lips touch the top of my head and his fingers glide up my back.

"Lotion me up?" I pass him the bottle of sunscreen.

Being a redhead, the term sun tanning is a foreign concept to me.

"I can't promise my hands won't roam." He sits up straighter, his legs on either side of the lounge chair making room for me between his thighs.

"You never do."

"And you love it."

I shrug because I have no complaints when the man I'm falling in love with can't stop touching me.

"Whoops." The tie of my bikini at my neck undoes and falls, leaving my breasts bare for anyone walking by us to see.

"Dax!" I cup my breasts.

He plants his lips on my neck, making a path down to the top of my shoulder. He plays me like a fine-tuned violin. "Shit, I just can't control them. They have a mind of their own." He undoes the string on my back and I'm left with the flimsy fabric of my bikini top in my hands.

I lean back into his chest, giving in to him. Why not, I have the same needs as him. Neither one of our wants ever wanes.

His large hands come around my middle, easing my own hands away, his own molding to my breasts and tweaking my nipples.

I run my own hands up and down his thighs, venturing up the edge of his board shorts.

"We should've stayed inside today," he whispers in my ear.

"You'd stay in every day."

"Damn right."

I feel his growing erection on my back and wetness starts to pool between my legs.

"Oh, excuse me." Eva backsteps away from the opening of the cabana.

Dax starts laughing while I'm sure I must look like I'm sunburned, my face feels so hot. I turn to give him an evil stare, standing and putting my top back on.

Once I'm decent, I sit in my own lounge chair. "Eva, I'm sorry. Come in," I call out.

The young waitress comes in, her face a matching shade of red to mine. "Here." She places the drinks down.

"Sorry, Mr. Campbell tends to be insatiable," I say.

She giggles, and Dax is busy looking at me like I'm the biggest buzzkill because I'm not in his lap.

"Eva, if you had that, wouldn't you be the same." He nods in my direction.

Eva seems a little uneasy, but she nods.

"Ignore him, Eva. Thank you."

"I can draw the opening if you'd like."

I'd take her up on her offer, but that would take away the view of the ocean.

"Great," Dax jumps at the chance.

"No, thank you. We're going to enjoy the view," I say.

"We are?" Dax drones.

"Yep. I'm about to make another deal."

Eva escapes probably thinking we're either about to fight or fuck.

"No more deals for us." Dax holds his hands up, taking a swig of his beer.

"You're telling me if I said we could make a deal where I'd blow you every day you wouldn't jump at that?"

"I'm not an idiot. But you want to make some stupid deal about how I can't touch you in the daytime or some crap. Not going to happen." He stares out at the ocean, his beer between his fingers.

"Do you think I could actually do that?"

He chuckles. "Well, I'm just putting it out there. I'll never agree to any no-sex deals."

"Note taken." I sip my margarita, eyeing him over the rim.

"What did your mom say?" he asks, changing the subject.

"You go from wanting to get lucky to bringing up my mom? Buzzkill, babe." I take an extra-large sip of my margarita.

My mom might never come around to Dax, but she's going to have to try if she wants to be a part of my life.

"She wants to be your coach. Said it's a family thing and since we're dating..."

There's only silence on the other side of the cabana. I sneak a peek at him and his jaw is hanging open, while he stares at me.

"Kidding." I wink.

He falls back in his chair, his hand clutching his heart. "Shit. Thank God."

"She's her usual self—bossy and irritable." I stir the straw around in my drink.

"Warning you about the evils of me, I'm sure."

"Nah. We made progress. You only came up ten times in the conversation." I laugh.

He chuckles, jumping to his feet and laying on top of me. "I'll win her over. Don't worry."

"I'm not." I wait for him to bring his face up to look into my eyes. "I don't care Dax. It's her problem if she doesn't like you and if she makes trouble for us, then she can get out of my life."

I know my mother and she'll never do that because Dax is right, he'll win her over.

He leans in and gives me a chaste kiss. "Can we draw the screen now?" he whines like a child.

"Okay," I relent, and he stands up, pulling the string and the fabric closes, shutting off the view, but giving us our privacy.

He starts at my toes, his hands running up my legs, past my knees and along my inner thighs.

My head falls back on the pillow, my hands gripping the sides of the lounge chair.

Dax's phone rings.

"Forget it," he mumbles, his lips millimeters from my center. Shivers follow in his path.

"What if it's something important?"

"Nothing is more important than what I'm about to do," he mumbles against my skin.

I try to relax again, enjoying his breath across my skin.

The phone rings again.

"We should see who it is." I feel for the phone on the other side of the table.

"I don't care." His fingers graze along the sides of my pussy, dipping under my swimsuit bottom.

I answer and listen to the news on the other end of the line. "Oh my God." I sit up and Dax's face lands on the chair with am oomph.

"Demi," he says, in his what the hell tone.

"It's Beckett, he broke his arm."

"What? How?" Dax doesn't get up but does lift his head, staring up at me.

"Grady says he slipped or something. Details are sketchy. He says he's fine and he's heading to Skylar's place to recover."

"Skylar's?" Dax's eyebrows raise just like mine. "She's cockblocking me from a thousand miles away," he mumbles.

I playfully kick his rib. "It's your friend."

He slithers up on top of me, taking my phone and placing it on the table. "And I love my friend, but there's enough of them to deal with him right now." He plants his head between the swell of my breasts and kisses the skin.

"Hmm...Beckett's staying at Skylar's." My mind starts wandering.

"Maybe now those two will figure out what everyone else already knows," Dax says and then continues to devour my breasts, pulling the bikini fabric away.

"I don't know, some people need a sledgehammer to fall on their heads to get it."

He glances up, cocking one eye my way. "I'm going to pretend you weren't talking about me."

"You go ahead and do that." I smirk.

"It's quiet time now. Shh."

I slide down my lounge chair letting him have his way. He pushes up on his arms, his four-leaf clover tattoo prominently on display. I run my fingers over it. I don't know if luck has anything to do with it, but sometimes things turn out so much better than you ever planned.

The End

COCKAMAMIE UNICORN RAMBLINGS

Sometimes when you're writing you just feel it—the chemistry between your hero and heroine. You can't stop writing them. You can't stop thinking about them. We wish this was true of all our books, but sadly it's not. Sometimes we struggle with the story or the characters while writing. With On Thin Ice, it was like magic pixie dust was sprinkled over our fingers while we typed. We became one with them, making this book a lot of fun to write. We hope you had as much reading it!

Fun fact, Rayne's husband is Korean. Korean-American. (It's so nice to be able to tell you personal things about ourselves now that our true selves aren't so secret.). So, she was able to tap in on some of the food, and language. Not that there was a ton in the book. If you haven't experienced Korean Barbecue, we highly recommend. So yummy! Other than though, research was our friend.

Oh and did you notice who won the hockey game??? CANADA...of course. Would Piper let us do it any different? Never. She was adamant that Canada *must* win gold in hockey. LOL

As you're watching Snowboard Cross this Winter Games, check out Nick Baumgartner, as he was a little of the inspiration behind Dax. And be sure to check out Alpine downhill skiing to see how fast those women zip down the hill like Demi did!

AS WITH ANY of our books, without the following people, we wouldn't be able to do what we love.

Letitia from RBA Designs for the amazing covers and for putting up with how nitpicky we can be.

Ellie from Love N Books for line editing. Thanks for putting on your MacGyver gloves because we put you in a tight spot once again. Thank you!

Shawna from Behind the Writer for her not only amazing proofreading, but also assisting us daily! We love you!

Social Butterfly PR for their top-notch organization of the entire Bedroom Games Series promo. We've adore working with you!

All the bloggers who carved out time to promote us and/or read and review the book. Thank you for selecting us to read when we know you have so many options. We're very grateful for the support!

All our early ARC readers, for wanting to get your hands on our words as early as possible. You keep us going.

And of course, all our unicorns. <3 What can we say? Now that we're out of the witness protection program, you've embraced us and we couldn't be happier to be able to share more of our *real* selves with you. We love you all soooo much!! Thank you for trusting us with your precious reading time.

Up next... Beckett Myers. You think he's all casual and

laid back, but you might be surprised once you get into his head. 😉

    xo,
    Piper & Rayne

ABOUT PIPER & RAYNE

Piper Rayne is a USA Today Bestselling Author duo who write "heartwarming humor with a side of sizzle" about families, whether that be blood or found. They both have e-readers full of one-clickable books, they're married to husbands who drive them to drink, and they're both chauffeurs to their kids. Most of all, they love hot heroes and quirky heroines who make them laugh, and they hope you do, too!

ALSO BY PIPER RAYNE

My Scorned Best Friend

My Fake Fiancé

My Brother's Forbidden Friend

The Baileys

Lessons from a One-Night Stand

Advice from a Jilted Bride

Birth of a Baby Daddy

Operation Bailey Wedding (Novella)

Falling for My Brother's Best Friend

Demise of a Self-Centered Playboy

Confessions of a Naughty Nanny

Operation Bailey Babies (Novella)

Secrets of the World's Worst Matchmaker

Winning My Best Friend's Girl

Rules for Dating your Ex

Operation Bailey Birthday (Novella)

The Modern Love World

Charmed by the Bartender

Hooked by the Boxer

Mad about the Banker

The Single Dad's Club

Real Deal

Dirty Talker

Sexy Beast

Hollywood Hearts

Mister Mom

Animal Attraction

Domestic Bliss

Charity Case

Manic Monday

Afternoon Delight

Happy Hour

Blue Collar Brothers

Flirting with Fire

Crushing on the Cop

Engaged to the EMT

White Collar Brothers

Sexy Filthy Boss

Dirty Flirty Enemy

Wild Steamy Hook-up

The Rooftop Crew

My Bestie's Ex

A Royal Mistake

The Rival Roomies

Our Star-Crossed Kiss

The Do-Over

A Co-Workers Crush

Printed in Great Britain
by Amazon

37275553R00101